BOY UNDONE

BOY UNDONE

Aaron Blackwood

Atlanta

CONTENTS

ACKNOWLEDGEMENTS

My sincerest and deep gratitude goes to the following people who helped manifest this book:

- Michelle Browne, my first editor who made this journey memorable. She was meticulous, generous, fun and always available.

- Katina Ferguson helped me with all stages of publishing, including designing this wonderful book cover. This brilliant super-mom is professional, intuitive, detailed and a writer in her own right of children's books.

- Marvin Heath, alias 'ayo'. He's a brilliant spoken word artist, writer, and poet.

- David Moody, my bestie, and most truthful critic.

- James Oputa, a very gifted young writer, and a tough critic.

CHAPTER ONE

t was one of those hot summer nights, with the kind of humidity that confuses the mind and weakens the body into laziness. Any form of cold water is the only source of relief. People mop their foreheads with it to cleanse sweat-bleeding pores. Young men remove stained T-shirts that cling to sun-tanned six-packs, and women wear less makeup and fret over body odors and sanitary taboos. Half-naked babies in pee-stained diapers cry on the shoulders of irritated mothers. Large crowds and lines are avoided at all costs; arguments—even more so.

I lived in three boroughs before I chose the one I liked most—Brooklyn. It is here, in my small one-bedroom apartment off Flatbush Avenue, that my story begins.

The loud humming of my air conditioner as it failed to adequately cool my cluttered bedroom woke me from an evening nap. The dryness of the air aroused my thirst, immediately followed by hunger and carnal stirrings demanding my attention. I satisfied the first two urges, and pondered how to fulfill the third.

I returned a few calls, then slipped into khaki shorts, a red tank top, and a pair of white Adidas sneakers. I hurried out the door to my car, making an excuse to myself that I just wanted to drive, get out for a bit; get some air. I knew full well that I planned to satisfy that third urge.

A gentle breeze validated my excuse, and made it unnecessary for me to turn on the A/C. I stopped turning the dial of the radio when I heard the smooth voice of Luther's latest hit single. I crooned along with him as my Mazda cruised the neighborhood, stopping at a Shell station to get gas. While filling up, I saw a succession of scantily-clad men heading in the direction of Prospect Park. They cautiously crossed the street, suddenly disappearing beyond the sidewalk, into the bushes and trees of the east side of the park.

I bought a soda, which I immediately opened at the register (under the disapproving eye of the Indian attendant), paid for it, and went to investigate. Being in the park that late at night was no longer really my thing, particularly after *the incident*. I said I would never go back there again, but tonight, an urge that strong talked me out of it. I was scared, or maybe more apprehensive—but at the same time, I was feeling adventurous. I promised myself that if I went in, it would only be a short distance, maybe amongst the trees closest to the road; not further in, like before.

I found the only parking spot under a street light, which concerned me a little. I would have preferred it to be a darker area because when I was done, I didn't want anyone seeing me slip back into my car. I got out of the Mazda and looked around before stepping onto the sidewalk, sipping my soda as I sought out a bench to sit on.

A light sweat had begun to collect in the crease of my back. A solitary drop crawled down my spine. There was no longer a breeze over here, and the air was humid. Strangely enough, it aroused instead of annoyed me. I resisted the urge to pull my tank top off and walk shirtless through the bushes, as I'd seen others do.

The moon was full and bright, seemingly almost in spitting distance, casting a muted glow on everything. It raised anticipation and excitement in me, but then a moment of déjà vu instilled fear. Cars drove by infrequently, scarcely drowning the high-pitched sounds of mosquitoes feeding in the air.

It felt good to know that my exams were finally over—at least for this semester. I thought that I'd done well, thanks to the help of professor McNabe—whom I imagined as my secret lover. I frequently entertained thoughts of quiet weekends at his cottage in the Hamptons, making passionate love until soreness and exhaustion set in. Snuggling under a red tartan blanket on his brown leather ottoman, or preparing dinner together, with light jazz playing in the background. Occasionally looking up from chopping vegetables, I would catch his smoldering glances from beneath thick eyebrows. But then I found out that he was engaged, and lost all interest in the tenured professor. It was just as well; I'd decided to take a year off school, because work was beginning to get hectic.

I eventually found a park bench sheltered in the shadow of a large oak tree. I finished my soda and tossed the can in the bushes—only to feel guilty about littering. I almost went to retrieve it, then heard the scurry of something moving in the bushes, and quickly changed my mind.

I dug deep in the folds of my pocket to retrieve a joint I'd put there earlier. I removed the foil it was wrapped in, meant to stifle the smell. Delicately rolled with my last piece of rolling paper, I now twizzled it between my thumbs and forefingers to straighten it out before lighting it with my blue Bic lighter. I inhaled slowly, allowing the first draw of smoke to embrace and invade my lungs, then held it for as long as I could before releasing it.

That first drag was like welcoming home an old friend with open arms and a smile. It satisfied, it soothed; it forgave. But this joint was a lot more pleasurable to me. An aphrodisiac, my precursor to sex, it prepared my body and mind to travel elsewhere, but in slow motion, making me more observant to detail and sensitive to the slightest touch, taking me to a totally different plane, free of worry. I took another drag and held it even longer, which made me cough–usually a sign of good weed.

Someone was approaching. I couldn't tell who it was, so I put out the joint on one of the weather-beaten wooden frames of the bench. The man approaching was slim, and walked with urgency to his step. He wore long, dark, loose pants and a matching short-sleeved shirt. As he got closer, I recognized his face.

I always saw this boy when out cruising, and for some reason, he couldn't stand me. When he got close enough to recognize me, he rolled his eyes and quickened his pace. I wanted to burst out laughing. He always had a nasty attitude towards me that I couldn't figure out. We had never even been introduced.

When he was out of earshot, I fell out laughing at the absurdity of him. The weed was kicking in. If I wasn't high, I would have taken his attitude personally, but in this state, I didn't give a shit. I laughed again, more loudly this time. I relit the roach, or what was left of it, and inhaled till the last remnants of it burned out.

I looked around for a prospect, but spotted none in the immediate vicinity. The weed was claiming me. As I adjusted my underwear, I felt a slight wetness around my balls from wayward pubic hair, causing me a little discomfort. My dick stiffened slightly, wanting to come out to play. It was ready. I shoved my hand down there and fondled it for a moment. I swear I could feel my heartbeat through it. I ran my fingers through the damp hair and brought my fingers to my nose to smell myself: the raw, musky smell of me and the faint aroma of Ivory soap. I chuckled at the thought that I was turning myself on.

After a short period of time, the weed fantasies in my head were interrupted by a faraway gunshot, shrugging me back to reality. I got off the bench and started to walk. A house music song played in my head, which reminded me of the great time I'd had at the club last week.

A black Jeep slowed down as it passed me. I saw a dark bald head turn to peer at me. The Jeep idled for a minute. I continued to walk, ignoring him, so he turned up his rap and sped off. *Hell no!* I thought. I was not going to be picked up like some common piece of trade. I turned the corner and continued walking along the sidewalk, adding a little swagger to my strut, like a thug.

This stretch of street before me was dark, and large trees behind the park fence provided perfect camouflage for the willing. Dark shadows moved in the bushes. I saw white sneakers, red shorts, white socks, yellow tank top, assorted colored baseball caps and light to dark-skinned bodies inhabiting this clothing. Their features were not distinct. The bodies moved slowly and sensuously, which excited me down below.

I was eager to participate, yet cautious. Suddenly a cell phone rang, startling me. The owner quickly silenced it, and had the nerve to answer it. "Hello…can't talk right now. Let me call you back." Someone else snickered.

I contemplated getting over my fears and venturing just a little further into the park.

Then it happened. Like a nightmare, a momentary flashback of *the incident* crossed my mind. Feelings of fear, humiliation and embarrassment smothered me. The blue lights. The flashlights…megaphone—the dogs. The handcuffs were on too tight; faces of shame in the police van, while others chewed gum, looking indifferent. "This your first time?" asked one of those boys. I nodded my head. "Thought so," he said. "It will be just overnight. You'll be out in the morning."

After an uncomfortable night on a hard bench with only a turkey sandwich and nasty coffee, he forgot to tell me that we'd be arraigned in court. That memory made me shiver.

But it was all behind me now. I had to live my life. I couldn't live based on *what-ifs*.

CHAPTER TWO

After repressing the guilty recollection, I slipped in and positioned myself amongst a cluster of trees that were close to the road, allowing me to clearly see anyone that approached. Streaks of light still pierced the darkness from the street. The occasional car would pass by and the peripheral light would briefly shed beams amongst the trees, revealing bodies engaged in contact. I resisted the urge to investigate, yet I felt compelled to do so. I felt caution stab me again, but assured myself that there was pleasure to be gained this time. The chase and capture of that first victim. My first prize of the night. My loins ached for that satisfaction.

These feelings were suddenly interrupted by a police car cruising by, pausing to view the group of suspiciously-parked vehicles along the road. My heart started beating faster. Feelings of regret enveloped my whole being. Slowly, the police car shot a large spotlight into the parked cars, and then into the woods. I heard movements around me duck in unison to the ground, and I followed with them.

Then came the sudden rustle of leaves and feet scampering on rough terrain, heading further into the park, and without thinking, I followed. I quickly followed a path into a large group of trees surrounded by thick bushes. I stopped and looked back, straining to see in the dark. There were no flashlights following or dogs howling. I leaned against a tree to catch my breath.

A mosquito bit me, and then another. I swatted at the invisible critters and tried not to scratch the itching wounds, which I knew would soon swell. Everything here was more aggregated;

only in clearings were rays of moonlight allowed through. I dared not venture out into the clearings. I convinced myself that I was not going to jail again, even if it meant camping out here all night, till the morning. I heard a rustle of leaves underfoot coming from a tree near me. I crouched down quickly, my heart beating fast.

Two men who weren't the police were a few feet from me. I strained to see what they were doing, so I moved closer. One was getting a blow job. They became aware of my presence. The one on his knees stood up; the other zipped up, and they moved on. I stood under the large tree, and waited for others to pass and maybe take an interest in me, or for me to reject them, if I wasn't feeling them. The lumps on my arm from the mosquito bites had swollen, and now teased me to scratch them.

All of a sudden, I sensed I was being watched. Not by many, but by one pair of eyes. I looked in the direction in which I sensed this energy or presence. A tall, slim, honey-colored man stood several feet to the left of me. He had on a thin-rimmed white beach hat, pulled down low just above his eyes. His loose-fitting, short-sleeved white shirt was unbuttoned slightly at the collar, above matching white slacks.

What an odd color to wear in here, I thought. Talk about attracting attention. I wasn't sure whether I was supposed to be scared of this ghostly figure or accept him as part of the scene tonight.

His arms were crossed over his chest, with the arm of his right hand raised, gently stroking his goatee. He appeared to be studying me. He stood perfectly still with the exception of his moving hand. His demeanor intrigued me and demanded my attention. I thought his stance unusual for this kind of setting.

The stroking of the goatee and the arms crossed over the chest reminded me of Professor Mc Nabe. That was something he would do. For a moment, my fantasy of the lovely professor flooded back, except that he was in the park, about to get his freak on. My hope of such a fate soon died, because the man in white was lighter than Professor Mc Nabe.

I stepped a little closer to see what lay beneath the low brim. He continued to stroke his goatee. I was at a loss for what to do next. I was out of my element. Total visible eye contact was somewhat restricted. In order to solve that, I would have to move closer to him. I didn't want to scare him off, so I stayed where I was, and let him make the next move.

At one point, he tilted his head, avoiding a beam of light that swept through the trees with rapidity that shocked us both. But it was only someone in the street making a U-turn in their car. The light from the car did briefly allow me to view his face. His eyes blazed with disgust at the irritation of the light. They looked like they might have been green. He was handsome, and looked Hispanic. He had a long, defined nose and thin lips. But it was the intensity of the eyes that sparked my interest.

A car door slammed. Someone else was exiting their vehicle and slipping into the park. The police must have moved on. I guessed they might not be doing a swoop tonight. I turned back to face my mysterious stranger in white, but he had disappeared.

Shit! That fucking dude slamming his door must have scared him off. Without hesitation, I decided to pursue him. Caution again sprang forth to remind me, but I ignored it. I presumed that the only direction he could have gone was down a makeshift path behind where he had stood. I eagerly followed the path with my suppressed fears.

I passed a very tall boy along the path. Not my type. Two guys with back-turned baseball caps and low hanging jeans were approaching swiftly. I panicked. I got off the path, hoping that they wouldn't follow me. They didn't, but continued on. I got back on the path, still slightly shaken. What if they'd tried to rob me?

Damn! I should never have come in here with my wallet. My friend Curtis had warned me to always have ID in places like this. God forbid being caught by the police or worse, dead for weeks, body unidentifiable. But in my sexual eagerness, I'd forgotten to leave the wallet in the car.

I rushed deeper into the park, but surprisingly, the trees and shrubs were not as dense, allowing moonlight to illuminate the dark. The hum of nature was in evidence, and the traffic some ways off seemed to have ceased. Maybe I had come too far from the action.

I was about to turn around when I saw the white presence of the man I sought, casually standing under a tree. He had his back to me. As I approached him, I heard him taking a leak. I stopped and waited for him to finish. But he was already aware of me. He turned around slowly, putting his dick away, but his hand was still within his fly, rubbing it.

Well, at least he's interested in me. I'm an old-fashioned guy; I would have liked conversation and dinner first, but look where we were. I figured I would have to move a little closer. As I approached him along the hastily contrived path, I slipped and fell.

I couldn't believe it. I was too embarrassed to get up or even look in his direction. I felt like such a fool.

I expected to hear him laughing. But he didn't. Instead, I felt a strong arm assisting me to my feet, and a soft, sexy voice say, "Are you okay?"

I looked at the concern in his eyes and furrowed brow. I couldn't move. Any pain from bruising from the harsh fall disappeared. I stammered back, "Oh... I'm okay, I guess."

"Are you hurt?"

"No, I don't think so." I checked myself for damage. "I'll be okay, I'll live."

I brushed myself off and applied a little spit to my bruised knee. He was still holding my half-raised body against himself.

He smiled. "I'm glad you're okay. You look like a handful to carry out of here." Then he quickly added, "a muscular handful," and smiled.

"You wouldn't have said that if I was thirty pounds heavier," I said.

"Yes, I would. I couldn't think of a lovelier load to carry." We both laughed at this lie.

As our laughter faded, I said to him, "You can let me go now."

He said, "Oh I'm sorry; I had gotten comfortable holding you. Your skin feels so soft." He licked his lips and rubbed a free hand on the arm of the mosquito bumps, just missing them. This man was really hitting me with bullshit lines, but I loved it. However, I didn't know how to respond to his last remark. All I could come up with was, "Come here often?" We both laughed again.

"No, I don't," he replied. "But I was on my way home and got sidetracked, and ended up here."

"I came out to get ice cream," I lied, "and also ended up here."

"It seems we both ended up here under questionable circumstances," he said, and smiled at me with a knowing wink.

"Possibly," I replied, knowing that I was still being vague.

"By the way, my name is Aidan," he said as he extended his hand.

It felt warm and firm. It fit in my hand perfectly. It was a regular handshake, instead of a dap, the hand-tapping guys normally do. I told him my name.

He said, "Pleased to meet you."

We both looked into each other's eyes. Our hands were still locked in the handshake. He seemed to communicate with his eyes. They had a gentle, kind look to them, as if they smiled. It reminded me of the bemused look of Leonardo Da Vinci's Madonna.

There was something else I detected in the way he looked at me. It was either a look of recognition or familiarity—I couldn't quite figure out which, but he looked startled at first.

"You seem familiar to me. I know we've never met, yet I feel like we have," he said.

"Maybe in a past life," I suggested with a chuckle.

"Maybe; anything is possible. There's something about your aura that I'm drawn to," he said, looking at me like he was seeing me in a different light. "You have a lot of light around you. Are you aware of that?" he asked.

"No. What do you mean?" I was at a total loss as to what he was talking about.

"I can see people's auras. It's hard to explain. But it's like a field of energy that surrounds every one of us. I sometimes can see them, and yours is dominated by reds and oranges."

He continued. "I don't know what that means exactly. To

explain it to you I would have to research it, but I do know that it's a good thing."

"Oh," I said, intrigued yet still confused. "You seem to be a spiritual man."

"I'm on a journey," he replied.

"A journey?" I said, a curious look on my face.

"Yes, a spiritual journey. One way of looking at it means that I'm open and aware to other ways of worshipping or knowing God, understanding why we are here, what we are here to do, and the best ways or decisions I should make to live my life."

I wasn't accustomed to discussing spirituality under these circumstances. But his outlook on life fascinated me. I surprised myself how open I felt towards learning more. Our conversation continued in this vein as I plied him with questions about his journey and what he had already learned or discovered. We must have talked for maybe a couple of hours before we realized that it was getting late.

CHAPTER THREE

hen our focus became physical. Our conversation fell to a more superficial level, redolent with sexual innuendo. I found Aidan very sensual. The smooth, slow, seductive way of expressing himself suited my waning high. I listened attentively as he spoke, turned on by his essence. An energy emanating from him silently touched and observed me at the same time. I felt like if he already knew me.

I pulled myself from the minor stupor, blaming my current state for this paranoia. I tried to direct all my attention to his features. I tried to stay in the moment and not let my imagination stray. I looked at his handsome face in the haze of the moonlight. To emphasize a point, his lips slowly moved in unison with his hands. It was then that I noticed a gold band on his left index finger. If he was married, that was something I didn't care for. But I was willing to look the other way, because he'd already reeled me in.

Aidan stopped talking and moved a little closer to me. He was a couple of inches taller than I was. I looked up into those beautiful eyes, which seemed to quietly whisper their dominance over me. The aroma of his musk brushed my senses.

"Do you know what I want to do with you?" he said.

"What?"

"I want to hug you."

No more was said. I wrapped my arms around his waist, while he wrapped his around my shoulders, and gently massaged my back and pulled me closer to him. His hug was firm, yet gentle at times. His warm body and musk engaged me as I nuzzled the right side of my face into the nape of his neck. We held each other without any groping. I hadn't been held like this in a very long time. I really needed this.

The light dampness made our skin stick slightly. I strained to smell him beyond his musk. I sunk my fingers into the lower cleft of his back, and ached to lower them, but didn't. In some strange way, I felt calm and fulfilled. What we were doing was enough. We didn't need to go further, which surprised me. I was content to hold onto this sweet-smelling man, here amongst nature, in the midst of night, while the moon softly looked on and celebrated, beams of subtle light blessing our union. I didn't want to let go. I refused to, and the wonderful thing was he did, too.

A sudden foreign movement forced us apart. Someone was approaching. It was a large, savage-looking light-skinned man in shorts, who had his shirt off. He stopped and watched us, reaching below his heaving belly, touching his crotch, and playing with a gold ring that hung off his large, dark nipple. He obviously wanted to join us.

Aidan whispered in my ear, "Let's go."

I reluctantly followed him deeper into the park, wondering why I trusted him so quickly. The man with the nipple ring was hot on our heels. Everywhere we went, he showed up, touching himself and swaying as his disgusting belly danced for us in the moonlight. After a while, this cat and mouse game became exhausting. Both of us instinctively knew that our stalker had no intention of leaving us alone. Eventually, Aidan led us back to the road. Once close, he stopped. So did our stalker.

"I think it's time to get out of here," he said.

"I know," I replied, disappointed.

"I would like to see you again," he whispered, his breath hot to my ear. He gently kissed it and looked down to me for an answer.

"I would like that."

"Here's my card. Call me in the morning when you get up. I will be waiting for your call." He pressed his card into my hand.

"Sure. I will," I said.

Then he hugged me one last time. This time, he held me tightly, like we were never going to see each other again. I closed my eyes, not wanting him to let go. But he did. It was sudden—and then he was gone. I opened my eyes to watch the white glow of his being disappear amongst the bushes in the opposite direction.

A cracking of a twig made me realize that our stalker was still present, looking like he was about to pounce in my direction. I turned abruptly and headed for the road.

I got in my car, still thinking of this mystical encounter with Aidan, my mind recounting every moment I'd spent with him. I started the car and pulled out into the road, not noticing till I got home that I'd gotten a ticket for illegal parking. I shrugged, threw it in the glove compartment, and went upstairs. Nothing was going to dampen the way I was feeling.

Once inside my apartment the silence of my living room made me rush to turn on the TV. I didn't want to be alone. Then thoughts of him comforted me. It took some time before I fell asleep, with I'm sure, a big smile on my face.

A few hours later, I awoke from what turned out to be a nap. Though it was short and I was tired, thoughts of Aidan spiritually invigorated me. I'd had a dream about him, but I couldn't remember the details, except that he hugged me—again. I relived the hug as I got myself together and started my errands.

I prioritized a list of things in my head. I called the Passport Agency to see if my passport was ready. It had slipped my mind to tell Aidan that I had a flight to catch this afternoon. I would have to call him and tell him that I was leaving town for a week.

The earnest nature of my trip now seemed inconsequential. I regretted having to leave him, knowing so little about him to sustain me in my absence. I bit into a warm blueberry muffin as I closed my apartment door, perplexed at the thought.

I've lived in Park Slope for three years now: a middle-class-to-upscale neighborhood filled with alternative types; artists, performers, activists and regular people of color who can or can't afford it. Gentrification is swiftly ravaging the neighborhood. Black people who rent or have homes here are being priced out with rising rents, mortgages, and property taxes.

The area is filled with gays, especially the ones who can no longer afford Manhattan—the island they call the Big Apple, across the Brooklyn Bridge. (I could never figure out why it was called that.) The pace here is slower than in frenetic Manhattan, with a more neighborly feel, possibly because of the huge, relaxing backyard called Prospect Park. One could get lost there and not see a soul—as I sometimes do, to get away from the masses of people that populate this busy city. Languishing under the protective umbrella of ancient trees is my only immediate escape from the summer's crucifying heat, a welcome refuge from all the heated concrete.

I lived on the second floor of a hundred-year-old brownstone. My landlord had renovated the second floor to include two separate apartments—small, but still cozy, especially when the heat rattled up through the pipes in wintertime.

Ron, a flight attendant, lived across the hall from me and was seldom home. When I did see him in the hallway, he was always slipping different men into his apartment, darting from the disapproving eye of Miss Lucy, the busybody of the building. She lived below me on the whole of the first floor, and was the longest-serving tenant. Her apartment was saturated with Harlem Renaissance antiques and pictures recounting her heyday. It was like a museum in there, and she loved being the curator of guided tours for anyone that was interested.

Miss Lucy was very, very old. When asked how old she was, she'd reply, "A lady never tells." Miss Lucy was prone to a drink or two. I could always tell when she'd had a nip by the odor that wafted behind her as she shuffled down the hallway. Whenever I came home and creaked up the hardwood stairs, the huge sliding doors from her apartment would peel open slightly, revealing her slow-moving right eye.

"It's just me, Miss Lucy," I'd whisper.

"Okay, baby," she'd respond weakly, and struggle to force the doors to slide back into place. With Miss Lucy around, we didn't need a security alarm system.

CHAPTER FOUR

rushed out of the Varick St subway to the passport agency, which was about a block away. I bypassed the line of people at the door and explained to the security guard that I was here to pick up my passport for a flight hours from now. He allowed me in without a hassle, and I went straight to the counter of the same representative, Angela, I had been dealing with. The process was swifter than I thought. We concluded business, and she handed me my first American passport with a mug shot that would make my own mother disown me.

Twenty minutes later, I was back in Brooklyn, finishing up my packing. I rummaged through the pockets of last night's discarded shorts to find Aidan's card. It was provocative, simple and unprofessional. A blank white card with raised black ink in italic font that read, *I am the man to meet all your needs.* On one side was a phone number, and on the other side was a website address. *Hmmm...I am the one to meet your needs. That's not professional. It sounds like the card of a hustler.*

I called him and waited anxiously for him to pick up. For some reason, I was feeling nervous. What would his voice sound like on the phone? I began to worry that my call would go to his voicemail, but he picked up after the fourth ring.

"What kept you?" he said, and with those words, I could almost see a sly smile.

"Morning errands."

"How are you feeling?"

"Tired."

"I'm sorry about that. I'll take a little of the blame for that."

"You don't have to."

"I'm glad you called."

"You thought I wouldn't?"

"I thought you would because we had a connection. But you never know these days. You know how you men are." And he laughed.

"I know what you mean, but I'm not one of those men," I fired back.

"Hmm. I see. I like that answer."

"It's true."

"No doubt. I'm sure you mean it."

"Did you get any sleep?" I asked, not able to come up with anything meaningful to say.

"I got a nap. But it was profound. I had a dream that gave me some clarity on an issue I was concerned about."

"Oh really. What was the dream about?"

"Maybe I'll tell you when I know you better. It was some deep shit."

"Okay. Just know I will remind you."

"Ah! A man that never forgets. I'm gonna have to watch you."

"Like you did last night," I teased.

"Yeah, I was studying you, wasn't I?"

"Yes, and it was intense."

"Oh, I'm sorry. I didn't intend to make you feel uncomfortable."

"You didn't. Nah! I'd be lying. Maybe just a little bit."

"Then, my handsome friend, I will try not to stare at you again. I don't want you thinking I'm some kind of crazy person."

"I don't think you're crazy. Just intense."

"I like that. I think that word sums me up rather well. I'll have to add it to my journal."

"Am I in there?"

"Oh yes. One of the first things I did when I came in was to add you to my book of secrets."

"You must have many to keep a journal on them."

"You have no idea, my friend…no idea."

I looked at the time, realizing I had to get off the phone and continue to prepare for my trip. I really didn't want our conversation to end, but it must.

"Aidan," I said his name for the first time. "I'm going out of town for a week."

"Where are you going?"

"England."

"Oh man. That's so cool. Pleasure or business?"

"Pleasure—well, sort of; family. Probably by the end of the week I'll be screaming to come home."

"Yeah, man. I know how family can be. Trust me on that."

"I look forward to talking and seeing you when I return."

"You have a date, my friend."

Before he hung up, he said he wished he could see me before I left. Without hesitation, I agreed that he should come over briefly to wish me bon voyage. One hour later, he hadn't showed. I was packed and ready to go. I started to write him a note when the doorbell rang. I ran down the stairs, excited to see him, if only for a moment. But the man that stood at my door was not the one I remembered meeting last night. He was white.

His skin was not olive-colored but tanned. His head was shaved bald, like a boiled egg. He wore a wrinkled shirt, stained slacks, and scruffy flip flop sandals. The look was totally East Village white boy – very "grunge."

I smiled to mask my shock. But I wanted the hot Puerto Rican that I thought I'd met last night. I smiled wider and took his extended hand. If he noticed my discomfort, he didn't let on. I invited him into the hallway of my building. In the dimness of the vestibule, his appearance returned to what was familiar. The intensity of his green eyes attacked mine, rendering me speechless for a moment—so much so that I forgot to release his hand. He indicated this with his eyes.

"Oh, I'm sorry."

"Why?"

"Your hand—"

"We've had this conversation, remember…the softness of your skin."

"Oh yeah, that's right." I laughed. An uncomfortable little chuckle.

"You were in my dream," he said.

"Oh yeah! So were…" I caught myself and stopped. This was too weird.

"You were saying?"

"I was saying, or about to say— do you remember it?"

"Yes, every wonderful moment of it."

He lowered his eyes when he said this and took me in. His inspection was intensive and thorough. When he was done, his eyes returned to mine. It trapped me in its attention. I scrambled for the right response, and to bring composure back to my voice and demeanor.

"Tell me about it," I asked.

"No!"

"Why not."

"Because," he paused. "The time is not right. I don't want to scare you off."

"Is it something spiritual, like the auras we talked about?"

A look of slight amusement lightened his features for a moment. That extended to a smile so brief that its after-effect lingered—a snatched memory of him I was to store away for future consumption.

"You don't want me to repeat myself, do you?"

"No," I retorted with a pinched tone. My instinctive inquisitiveness was silenced into embarrassment. To hide my shame, I turned and headed for the stairs, indicating that he follow me. Over my shoulder, I informed him that I was taking the train to the plane. He kindly offered to give me a ride to the train station. The last flight of stairs, we did in silence.

How could I have missed this? His voice hadn't given him away. He had the kind of vernacular that could have passed for either race. How the hell could I have been so foolish? But more importantly, how do I get rid of him?

We stepped into my apartment, and his reaction was exaggerated but complimentary. He beamed and spun around in awe at my apartment. He especially liked the exposed brick walls that ran along both sides of the apartment, right into the bedroom. He seemed knowledgeable of the architecture of the space. He said it was similar to a job he was currently on. I guessed that explained his attire and why he smelled of paint.

He gave himself a quick tour of the space. His vocabulary was repeatedly spiced with the exclamation "Wow!" as he peeked into the open doors of my bathroom and bedroom. He wanted to know how long I had lived there, and did the owner have similar properties? He ran his fingers along the grain of the kitchen countertop, identifying what kind of wood it was, and then he stopped.

"Now it's my turn to be sorry."

"For what?" I asked, thinking, this man is sorry a lot.

"I should be focusing on you."

When he said those words, something in me stood still. What a nice thing to say. The sincerity of the thought was in his eyes; there was no mistaking it. I knew bullshit when I saw it. This was not that.

"You are beautiful," he said as he took a step into my aura, our noses inches apart. I was not expecting another compliment, even though inappropriate and unconventional, maybe even insulting. I was not beautiful. I was kind-of-average, definitely not a head-turner, but I took it in the spirit that it was probably meant, because it also carried sincerity with it.

I felt trapped again, as in the hallway. I wanted to remain, but I had to pull away. I had to break the spell. Uncomfortable, I was about to avert my eyes when he gently took my chin and held it, bringing the focus right back to where it had been. That look of familiarity that I saw in the park returned as we stood there looking at each other—only he looked as if he were examining my face. I was forced to look at him with unease. He smiled at me—the same smile that had disarmed me in the hallway. It relaxed me. Comfort replaced discomfort.

My embarrassment at such an intimate exchange, if only with the eyes, also succumbed to his essence. Something was being exchanged between us on a telepathic level. In those moments, my prejudice adjusted, replaced by curiosity. My physical desire for him last night had now morphed into something else, like that of a new gadget or animal that one would have to get used to. How was I to deal with being with a white man? What would my friends think? What would strangers think—particularly other gay guys?

He hugged me briefly, before I cut it short because I had to go. But while it lasted, I could feel his heart beating fast. The chemistry of our bodies coming together seemed to give off some kind of reaction that excited me, forcing me to pull away, because I couldn't explain it. It was intensely different. Maybe the paint fumes had something to do with it. Was it because I had never been with a white man before? This wasn't what I wanted. This wasn't what I prayed for. What the hell was going on?

We grabbed the bags and headed downstairs to his car. My eyes widened as I stared at the anomaly parked in front of my building. He had an ugly old car—so old that I wasn't familiar with the make. The seats were covered in blankets for his dog. There was junk on the floor in the back.

Just then, I envisioned always having to brush dog hair from my clothing, carrying a little spray bottle of cologne to mask the smell, and always washing my hands. As he cleared away junk to make room for me, he said the dog had urbanized his car. I prudently got in the car and immediately noticed parts of the roof lining had been ripped off. He noticed my shocked expression.

He just said, "The dog."

"Where is it?"

"Oh, she's at home. It's too hot for her to be out now."

After a couple of false starts, the engine sputtered into action, and slowly, the car lurched forward. I was thankful that the station wasn't far, because in this thing, we would never make it. This piece of junk was definitely on its last legs.

On the way to the station we passed an abandoned building in the Fort Greene area, which was a mixed community of progressive blacks, whites, artists, and gays. He mentioned doing the research on the building to fix it up. I asked him if he had backers to do such a project. He simply said the he had done it before. I thought of the words on his card and chose to ask no more.

At the station he assisted me with my bags out of the car. When his back was turned, I quickly brushed off dog hairs that clung to my pants.

"How long will you be gone?" he asked.

"Seven days."

"That's a long time. I am already counting the minutes."

Is this dude for real? That is the corniest line in the book.

"I'll be back before you know it."

"It always seems to happen to me. I meet someone and they get yanked away." He looked away when he said this, as if recalling a memory.

"I will call you," I said.

"I would like that, very much."

With his engine still running, we exchanged a brief goodbye and shook hands, our eyes never leaving each other's. As I boarded the train, the words on his card were in my head, as if I'd memorized them: *I am the man to meet all your needs.*

CHAPTER FIVE

transferred to an airport bus to take me to my terminal of departure. I was fascinated by the variety of nationalities represented in the bus—all going to different parts of the world to continue, visit, or start a new life.

In the departure lounge, thoughts and concerns about Aidan still in my head, I called my best friend David to ask his opinion.

"David, I met this boy in the park—"

"I thought you were going to stay out of there."

"I know, but I couldn't help myself. You know how it is.

"Know this, I'm not bailing you out again."

"I'm sorry, but I was horny."

"Damn, Isaiah! Go to a bathhouse or peepshow. Someplace safe."

"I will next time. But I really need your advice."

"What is it?"

"When I met him, I thought he was Puerto Rican, but he's not. He's white."

There was silence on the other end of the phone. I could have sworn I heard David sigh. "How come you didn't know that in the first place?" he asked.

"Because we met in the moonlight, but when I saw him in the daylight, it was obvious. I'd made a mistake."

"What are you going to do?"

"I don't know. That's why I'm asking you."

"You don't like that he's white. I don't see a problem. Just don't see him again."

"But—"

"But what?"

"I like him."

"Will that be enough?"

"I don't know."

"He makes you uncomfortable. Have you noticed if he feels the same way?"

"No. I hadn't thought of that?"

"You'll have to figure that out with him. Watch his actions, listen to his words. You'll know."

My flight to Manchester, England would take six hours and fifty minutes. It was cramped and uncomfortable, but for some reason, that didn't bother me. I was feeling happy, looking out onto an infinite expanse of clouds. I was able to think and reminisce on random things in my life.

I was on my way to see my family. My absence has been long. I had moved and stayed away to avoid the questions, the prying, and the opinions on my private life. The expectations they had of me were too great. They suffocated me, so I ran and didn't look back. My communication had been minimal. It was unfair of me to do that to them because of my own fear of being found out, of being a fraud, and pretending to be someone I wasn't.

Most of all, I terribly missed my grandmother, who we called Mama. She was like my second mother, the woman I bonded with as a child, instead of my own mother. In her care, I came to know what love was. In her house, it was never denied to me. She stood by me when others wouldn't. She spoiled me, but also disciplined me when necessary.

I grew up having great respect for my elders. Never would a harsh word towards them leave my lips —even though I sometimes felt otherwise in my heart. I ran in order to not face that confrontation and have to disrespect them by being my truth. I didn't know what this trip would bring—but in some way, I wanted to make amends.

As I ate the flavorless chicken casserole the steward laid before me, thoughts of Aidan kept popping up in my head. I analyzed every aspect of him that I'd been exposed to so far. I questioned why he was in my thoughts so prevalently, and so soon. I worried about our differences. He being white was a new obstacle that bothered me, making me question if I was a racist to feel that way. David's advice played mediator to my thoughts.

The more I tried to push him out of my mind so I could focus on a movie, the more present he became. I realized I was really enjoying thinking about this man. Eventually, I surrendered to those thoughts as I closed my eyes, propping a pillow behind my neck, attempting to sleep.

I did not sleep well, especially with a large lady sitting next to me, who pushed me further towards the window as her sleeping head tried to rest on my shoulder. When we landed, I welcomed the first real opportunity to stretch my legs and quickly headed to Customs.

At the arrival lounge, Aunty Brenda and her son James were there to meet me. She swept into my arms, remarking how I'd changed. She looked the same, with her windswept hair piled on top of her head in her trademark chignon. She had aged a little, though. Plump laugh lines shielded her generous upper lip. There was a tiredness there, probably due to self-induced stress, which she unconsciously welcomed and complained about at the same time. Her tall, slender body looked wonderful in a flowery blue summer dress with matching flats.

My cousin James hadn't lost his baby fat. Aunty Brenda always described him as a thick boy with the perfect body for rugby. She would never admit he was overweight due to her overfeeding him. James gave me one of those firm, manly handshakes that hurt.

"How is Mama?" I asked, retrieving my crushed hand from his vice-like grip.

"The same," responded Aunty Brenda as she searched my features, as if confirming the changes.

"She's a trooper," piped in James.

"She will be very glad to see you. You're all she talks about," Aunty Brenda sneered. "How long has it been?" And before I could answer, she cut me off with a scathing edge to her voice. "Too bloody long. You should be ashamed of yourself, Isaiah…"

she scolded. Well, that didn't take long. I knew her congeniality was a ruse before the attack.

"Mum, calm down. Don't cause a fuss," James chided his mother.

"I'm not causing a fuss. It's been so long since he's been to see us, he can't even remember." She was getting agitated. I hugged her to stifle all that anger. She held onto me for a moment, then pushed me away.

"Come on, let's get to the car."

We piled in her old weather-tarnished white Volkswagen. I sat in the back seat while James drove, and she sat next to him, and over her shoulder, she filled me in on the latest family drama. I watched cows grazing in rich green fields as the car hurtled deeper into the English countryside, and Aunty Brenda prattled on about stuff she had already told me on the phone countless times in the past few weeks.

In the midst of her vitriol about my grandmother's ungratefulness, my mind drifted to Aidan. I remembered his smile, snatched up and tucked away in my head. His fascination with the unknown. The way his hand cupped mine perfectly. The gentle kiss planted on my ear before we bid farewell.

"Are you listening, Isaiah?" Aunty Brenda had turned around and was staring at me with suspicious concern.

"Yes, Aunty Brenda. I'm just a little tired." James gave me a knowing look through the rear-view mirror that said, *You know Mum.* I certainly did. His mother resumed her nagging where she'd left off.

Finally, we arrived at Aunty Brenda's red brick home amongst a cluster of similar-looking others in her sub-division. Her deceased husband had built it from scratch for her and their impending family decades ago. Mama was already at the open front door, waiting to greet us. She looked like she wanted to cry, but was forcing herself not to. She'd lost a lot of weight. She no longer had the robust energy and girth of her youth, and her grey hairs had multiplied since I saw her last. She stepped down from the one-step stoop and made her way towards me, her movements a little hesitant and unbalanced.

Holding my grandmother in my arms reminded me of life's cruel reversal of fate. Thirty-odd years ago, she held me to her bosom, where I always knew that everything would be okay. Now today, it was my turn to hold her to mine, but I could not guarantee her that all would be well. The stroke had affected her mobility. Her sight and hearing had diminished considerably. She had just been diagnosed with diabetes.

The ravages of time had begun to take hold of a body that had been a worthy nemesis. Time was now winning, and she knew it. Her salt-and-pepper hair was mostly salt now, and it suited her. It made her look like a distinguished dame. She was the mighty doyenne that had outlived all of her friends, her husband, and four children. She survived on memories no longer taken seriously by the youth that surrounded her.

They were more concerned with her imminent death than the sagacious gifts she had to offer. I looked in her eyes and saw loneliness there—hiding. I held on to Mama as she softly cried on my chest, with tears of joy and sorrow. Mine were of regret and forgiveness.

At dinner that night, the whole family was gathered. The prodigal son had returned. All was forgiven—well, at least for tonight. My family held grudges, and it was only a matter of time before I would be reprimanded for my indifference and absence. Aunty Brenda had already started her revenge in the car.

The girls—my two cousins—had grown into lovely young English women of color. My mentally challenged Aunty Rhea would rock back and forth in her chair, and rush to clutch me at every opportunity.

These unscheduled interruptions from Aunty Rhea always came with her request for toiletries. She had the mind of a child in the body of an old woman. It was from her that I learnt what unconditional love was. I think she took a liking to me, because I was patient with her. When everyone else either ignored, dismissed or scolded her, I waited as she stammered out words, or swung her arms frantically to convey a point or feeling. In her eyes, I could do no wrong, and all I did was wait and listen.

Mama watched me quietly from across the dining table. I knew she was seeing the little boy that she treated like her own. Aunty Brenda barked orders and shoveled food into plates that needed it, always putting herself last, as usual. What would they think if they knew? I could never bring a boyfriend home to be a part of this. I could never bring Aidan to this. I was surprised that I could even think that far ahead, to imagine a white boy fitting in with my family.

Later on that night, I finally had to excuse myself from hearing regurgitated stories of my childhood forced upon me. I passed Mama's room and looked in on her. She was asleep, her head in curlers tied up in a bright scarf. She snored quietly, and looked so peaceful. I feared the day that she would not wake up from such peace.

Turning off James's bedside lamp—whose room I had stolen for my stay—I thought about Aidan and what he must be doing at the moment. *Is he thinking about me?*

The next morning, Aunty Brenda poked her head in to announce breakfast, and scared me with a green face mask and pink curlers, tied with a matching sheer rag.

At breakfast, I was informed of my itinerary for the next six days. James gave me one of those *I pity you* looks.

The next few days, I attended museums, amusement parks, and shopping malls, none of which I had an interest in. They only knew the boy that I was, and not the man I had become. The probing into my private life had already begun, as everyone took turns in inquiring about a girlfriend, marriage, or potential grandkids. It irritated me, and I dodged unrelenting interrogations with vague answers or fabricated promises. I began to count the days for my return to New York, and Aidan.

I had called him a couple of times already, but only got his answering machine. I did not leave a message. I didn't want to appear desperate. Protocol demanded I wait at least three days before calling. I had already broken that. I was relieved that he didn't answer, but at the same time, I longed to hear his voice.

The old adage "absence makes the heart grow fonder"—which an old boyfriend had once given me in a Hallmark card, and which I scoffed at, probably because I didn't feel the same way about him—now truly meant something, yet I was still baffled at its sudden appearance. On my fourth attempt to reach him, he picked up the phone.

"Hey baby, how's your trip going?" I was a little surprised by such a familiar greeting so soon.

"If I said I was having a good time, I would be lying."

"Is your family getting on your nerves?"

"Yep!"

"I understand, babe." He did it again. "Anything I can do?"

"Can you come and get me?"

He laughed out loud. "I would love to. Do you think your family would mind if we slept in the same bed?"

"I think it would be a real problem."

"They don't know?"

"No. They don't."

There was silence on the phone for a moment as he digested that bit of information. "They know," he said.

"No, they don't!" I almost shouted at him.

"Why are you being so defensive?"

"Because you don't know my relationship with them."

"But don't you think at this age in your life that they may have figured it out? Mine did."

"I don't know your circumstances, and for you to presume that—"

"Are we having our first argument?" he interrupted. There was amusement in his voice. I realized then that he was intentionally baiting me. He had pushed my buttons, and was seeing how far I would go.

He did make me mad and defensive, but he defused it in that last sentence. I had become a 'we' to him. I had become a 'baby' and a 'babe' to him. It felt odd to know that he was feeling the same about me as I struggled not to feel about him.

"I guess we are," I responded.

"I miss you."

Those words made me uneasy. Why should these three words mean anything at this point in our friendship?

"Did you hear what I said?" he interrupted the silence on my end.

"Yes. I heard." I didn't want to show my true feelings at this time—it was too soon. I had done this in the past, and it didn't work. It scared them away.

"You don't have to answer that," he continued. "I tend to say what I feel, and it's gotten me in trouble many a time. But this is who I am, and I won't hide that side of me."

"I understand," I responded, kicking myself for being so vague, but at the same time, enjoying not being the one to pour out my feelings first.

"I have a client in the other room waiting on me, so I have to get back to him, but before I go, I have a favor to ask."

"What?"

"I want you to repeat after me." And he went right into it. "I can't wait to see you when I get back. You have also been on my mind. I might like you, Aidan."

I smiled inside. I think every cell in me was smiling. Someone else was taking the initiative. I didn't have to do the work; just sit back and be adored.

I started to honor his request.

"I can't wait to see—"

"Stop!" he said suddenly. "I want you to say it as if you mean it. Not in that monotone voice you were doing."

I wanted to say something smart at that comment, but I resisted the temptation. The image of his smile popped into my head, and from my lips, I uttered the words he wanted to hear—but this time, I think I really meant them.

"That's what I'm talking about!" he shouted. He sounded like a brother when he said it. I laughed, and he laughed with me, creating a union between us that needed no words. I hung up the phone, our laughter still ringing in my ears.

I got up to go back downstairs, but suddenly stopped. I saw Mama's back slowly turning to close the bedroom door I was in. I froze. A spasm of fear ran through me like lightning. My happy mood disappeared, replaced by anxiety so severe, I could feel it upsetting my stomach.

CHAPTER SIX

had not been aware of her presence. How much did she hear? Did she have her hearing aid on? I sat back down to allow her time to get downstairs. Would she tell Aunty Brenda? Did she know I was talking to a man?

I remained in my room for the rest of the night, afraid and too ashamed to face the others. I was sure she had told Aunty Brenda, because no one knocked on my door to ask me to come down. I could hear laughter downstairs; were they laughing at me because they already knew? I cracked the door to eavesdrop. They were watching a sitcom on TV. Maybe she hadn't told them yet. Knowing Aunty Brenda, by now she would be at my door, confronting me.

I closed the door and picked up the novel I'd brought on my trip, hoping to lose myself in James Patterson's latest adventure of intrigue and espionage. But the exotic locations and twists and turns of the plot could not hold my attention. Frustrated, I turned off the light and tried to sleep.

"You want any supper, luv?" Aunty Brenda said suddenly from behind the closed door.

"No, Aunty Brenda. I'm not hungry"

"Are you sure, luv?"

"Yes, I'm sure. I'm just a little tired from jet lag. I will see you tomorrow."

Hoping this would dismiss her, I realized I had slipped into a British accent, which was the norm when I was around them. They sometimes joked about it, saying it sounded like a typical American trying to fake a British accent.

"All right, luv. I'll see you tomorrow. Don't forget, we'll be leaving early for Liverpool to avoid the traffic."

"Okay! Goodnight."

"Goodnight, luv."

I knew she wanted to come in to talk, but I couldn't deal with her right now. I also knew that Mama hadn't told her anything, because she wouldn't be calling me "luv." Avoiding coming out to my family definitely had its drawbacks. I guarded my privacy from them with some hostility, making them feel defensive on the subject. Separated by absence and the Atlantic Ocean, it had worked for a number of years.

I never lied. I just manipulated the truth—occasionally mentioning a friend as if he were female, then quickly substituting a similar thing I had done with one of my female friends, so as not to feel bad, or that God would punish me for lying to my family.

I had no intentions of coming out because I felt I didn't have to. Now, this unforeseen circumstance was forcing me to prepare another excuse for when the shit hit the fan. In frustration and to settle my nerves, I changed my focus to Aidan, and it worked. Before I drifted off to sleep, it struck me how quickly feelings for this stranger had developed, even though I still hadn't decided what to do about him.

I had a dream, and Aidan was in it. It wasn't clear and I only remembered bits and pieces. I saw us laughing somewhere…it could have been a restaurant or someone's home. We were at a dining table, because there was food prepared ready to eat. Then the scene switched to us embracing. It wasn't passionate; it was something else, kind of urgent, and it felt like I was holding on to him for dear life. Then I saw him waving goodbye and fading away…like in a haze or something. I was crying, and I did not wave back. That was all I could remember.

After waking from this troubling dream in the middle of the night, I went to use the bathroom. I thought about it briefly, then discarded it, thinking my dreams never came true or made sense, and went back to sleep.

The next morning, I avoided Mama at all costs. The couple of rosaries she wore around her neck tinkled as she moved, and her slow, shuffling movements around the house always gave me a heads up on her whereabouts. When we were ready to leave, I shouted goodbye to her from the bottom of the stairs and headed swiftly for the door. She did not respond, which was unusual, because I said it loud enough so that she could hear, even without her hearing aid on.

We did a lot of sightseeing in Chester and Liverpool, the latter of which included a mandatory visit to the Beatles museum. I really wasn't interested in the Beatles or their history, but this was what they wanted to do, so I pretended to care. Their attitudes toward me had not changed, yet I feared when they would.

My cousin Olivia had joined us, and at dinner, she chattered on about her new job and boyfriend "Rob." She was thrilled about this man; she practically glowed. Aunty Brenda listened with the cautionary perspective of a mother, realizing that her daughter was entering another phase of growth—something she was not ready for, because she liked how she was before puberty; dependent on her. Not a woman yet. Not ready to leave home yet.

James joked with his sister about Rob's poor handling of syllables and thick east end accent, which she ignored, being used to her brother's silly sense of humor. She had grown into a beautiful young woman, with lips that made her the envy of her friends—she looked like a black Angelina Jolie. In her joy, I saw mine awakening with similar feelings for Aidan. I understood, and smiled encouragement to enjoy this feeling for Rob, even as I masked my own for Aidan.

Before supper, that night I tried to call Aidan, making sure the door was securely shut and that Mama was downstairs. I got Aidan's answering machine, but left no message. I wanted to share with him what had happened, and maybe get advice on how to handle it.

Mama was making dinner when we came in. She listened to Aunty Brenda's account of our trip in silence, casually glancing my way when my name was mentioned. I retreated to my room, bothered by this lack of attention, contrary to what she had lavished on me when I first arrived. She must have heard something. There was no other way to explain her behavior.

I had dinner in my room alone that night, with some protest from my aunt. I picked up my book and quickly fell into James Patterson's world. On a full stomach, I must have dozed off. I awoke to the gentle prodding of a stick. Through fuzzy vision, I saw it was Mama poking me indignantly with her walking stick.

"Wake up, boy," she said, sounding like her old self.

"Mama? Wassup?"

"Huh?"

"I mean, what's wrong?"

"Nothing is wrong with me, boy. The question is what is wrong with you?" Oh lawd, the shit was about to hit the fan, and I was not fully prepared.

"What do you mean?"

"Your attitude. You haven't seen us in years, and you spend most of your time alone in this room or on the phone." I breathed out a sigh of partial relief, knowing that I wasn't fully in the clear yet.

"Mama, I've been tired a lot, and…"

"Boy, don't give me that. You're a young man. Who knows how long till we see you again, or if I'm alive when you do." Those last few words hit me hard. I couldn't imagine seeing her in a coffin. I moved towards her and gently embraced her.

"I'm sorry, Mama. You're right. I have been selfish."

She framed my face with both her wrinkled hands, and through sapient eyes, looked at me like she used to when I was a kid.

"You're my first grandchild. The first is always special. You know I love you, boy. I worry about you like if you were my own—probably more than that wicked mother of yours." I smiled and cupped her hands which were sprinkled with veins and moles, but had strength in their coarse grip. Her words brought me comfort, and I was very grateful for them, like a blessing. We sat in silence for a while. In the past I always had or knew what to say to her. Now I was clueless.

"Do you remember your Aunty Willie?" she asked.

"Yes, of course. I think about her sometimes. I miss Aunty Willie."

"I miss her, too." There was something in her tone that made me look at her. She had a distant look of confusion mingled with love and regret.

"They talked about her, too. But I didn't care. She was my special friend." She rose to leave, and the confusion on her face settled into love as she looked at me before slowly navigating her way out of the room with her stick.

I sat stunned, totally bewildered by what she had just said. In a few words, she had said so much, but with ambiguous implications. I slowly began to piece together what she had said in my head to make the most logical scenario, based on what history I had.

Aunty Willie had been Mama's good friend. She was not really my aunt, but a neighbor that lived down the road. She was a strict woman who had become my grandmother's confidante, particularly when my grandfather was away from home, drinking or chasing other women. In his absence I had heard her urge Mama to leave the man many a time. Aunty Willie was not an attractive woman; some would say 'manly.' She always looked awkward in a dress and heels, and would stiffen up when taking a picture, looking like she was about to attack the camera.

She never married. They found her alone, dead. Mama had gone into a period of mourning, and for months, was not herself. I had heard other family members insinuate rumors about Aunty Willie, but I never knew what they meant.

Now I thought I knew—was Mama telling me that Aunty Willie was a lesbian, and she didn't care then, nor did she care now what I was? Was Mama and Aunty Willie more than just friends? No, that couldn't be, because she said that 'they talked about her, too.' Oh shit! *That means they had already been talking or were suspicious of me.* But who?

I began to dissect my behavior around them, trying to figure out what I may have said or what mannerisms that may have slipped out and given me away. I felt now like I did when I was first called a 'faggot' at one of my jobs by this ignorant co-worker that I couldn't stand. I thought nobody knew; I was humiliated. He made me feel worthless, like a piece of shit. That was how I felt now—that my ruse to the world had been discovered, but nobody bothered to tell me that the game was up. How foolish of me to think that my façade could go on forever without question.

It was now, in my dismay, that I needed Aidan's arms to hold me. I wanted to cry, but couldn't. All these years of suppression, and I couldn't find a way to release it. I could feel rage and anger in my gut, like I had eaten something abrasive and it was cutting up my insides.

I had been hiding from myself for so long that I didn't know how to come out, or want to. It was safe being who I was—or what I had come to believe I was. I feared the judgment of others. I didn't want to be different. In my eyes, I wasn't. Being gay was something that I took out to play on a whim…when it was safe.

I had a hard time falling asleep that night. I don't think I really did; my mind wouldn't let me.

For the rest of the trip, Mama went back to treating me as normal. I became aware of how precious she treated each moment in my presence. How our conversations with each other were now effortless and comfortable. I spent a hilarious afternoon with her as she tried to teach me how to bake bread and cook chicken. She quickly became aware that her cooking skills were not one of the traits I had inherited, but she made light of it and scolded me into shape without the use of the word 'boy', instead calling me by my name. I think she was finally coming to terms that I had grown up and become a man.

CHAPTER SEVEN

ack in New York in the midst of rush-hour, I took the subway home. I made a mental note never to do that again. Next time, I should ease my way back in the city by having someone pick me up. The next few days were spent returning to work and getting caught up on what I had missed. My team at work had already embarked on a new project and started work on the website. I didn't really care for it, and after a preliminary viewing, neither did the client. I had to flog the whip to get the team on the same page, so we could produce a stellar website for our client's launching campaign.

Even with all the catching up I had to do for all aspects of my life, Aidan was constantly on my mind, and I couldn't wait to see him. Unfortunately, he was out of town, at his parents' in Connecticut. Due to some unforeseen issues with his parents, what was supposed to have been a weekend there turned into a few days more, without a leave date set. He didn't elaborate on what that was, and I didn't ask.

We spoke every day, usually more than once. In this way, I began to learn about this man. He was easy to talk to, and he opened me up to sharing much of myself. He seemed particularly interested in my holistic eating habits, and asked me lots of questions about it. He said he planned to change much of his diet to more fruit and vegetables, except for the meat. He was a carnivore, and no way was he giving that up for meat alternatives.

I looked forward to our long sessions on the phone. I could always tell when he was lying down to talk to me. His voice was deeper, more relaxed, and I could feel him listening intently as I prattled on about my job, about New York, and other trifling matters; general complaints that made me wonder if I was turning into my mother. God, I hoped I wasn't nagging him. Once comfortable with someone, I did have a tendency to be chatty.

I attempted to listen more and engage him with questions to know more about him. His answers sometimes felt censored, or he would tell me he didn't feel comfortable talking about that yet. One of the subjects that was off limits was his ex-lover.

"Aidan, whenever I've asked you about him, you've had very little to say or changed the subject. I've told you about all my past boyfriends."

"You chose to tell me. Sometimes a little more than I want to hear."

"What are you saying that I talk too much?" I knew I did, but I wanted to see what his response would be.

"Isaiah, all I'm saying is that some things are best left unsaid, particularly when it comes to past loves."

"So, you are saying I talk too much."

"No, Isaiah." He was getting a little agitated now. "I've learnt that such things can come up and be used against a person—say, for example, if they got into an argument."

"Have you experienced this?"

"Once. It was tense. It changed things."

"Was that with the ex-lover?"

"Like I said, I don't want to talk about him. That was the past. I don't want to relive it by telling you."

"I'm sorry. I'm just trying to get to know you."

"I know. Then know me. Not my past."

What ever happened between them was still painful for him. I could feel the wall of resistance through the phone. Not knowing about the ex-lover was hard for me. I feel that he was the key to knowing why Aidan shut down when I brought it up. Something happened between them, and left Aidan deeply scarred.

Finally, a week later, Aidan called and said he'd be returning later that day, and would visit me tonight. I couldn't wait. I was so excited to see him. I spent most of the day cleaning my apartment—I didn't realize how much I'd neglected its maintenance. I was so exhausted when I was done that I took a two-hour nap before his arrival.

Around eleven o'clock, the bell rang, and I buzzed him up. He looked better than I remembered. We caressed each other tightly. I nuzzled my nose against his. He rubbed my back with his strong, thick hands. I loved that he did that. We pressed our hips closer together. I was instantly hard, and felt his erection competing against mine. We gently kissed. At first, our noses seemed to get in the way—or at least the angle in which we held our heads and approached each other's lips.

It took a little getting used to, maybe because his lips were thinner than mine, and the hint of garlic on his breath initially restrained me. I thought that maybe he wasn't a good kisser, and our lips might be mismatched. But as we got into it, I was able to slide my tongue deeper into his mouth. He loosened his jaw and surrendered to this aggressive intrusion.

It felt different than kissing a black man, but I wasn't sure in what way. We were feeling each other out, and as each hurdle got conquered or deflated, I was sure that there were more differences to come. He touched my dick, then stroked it through the thin mesh of my long basketball shorts. He said our dicks were the same, indicating that I could touch or see his. I didn't want to see it then, because I was enjoying the intimacy of just touching through our clothes, but I felt it anyway. It surprised me—it was thicker and longer than I would have thought. I squeezed the head, which was as hard as a clove of garlic. It was trapped by his shorts and underwear, pointing downwards at an angle along his thigh.

Still holding each other, I led him to the sofa, whispering softly to him as we touched intimate areas with the tips of our fingers. He aggressively pulled me to sit on his lap, causing me to nestle the crack of my butt in his crotch. For a moment, he held me and hugged me closer to him. I wondered about his preference in bed. I thought he was versatile, maybe? Whatever he was into, we would work it out.

It was at this point he reached over to his bag and pulled out a card. A coarse piece of thread tied the card together, which was really a blank index card folded in two. He handed it to me. I untied the thread and opened it. Inside, on the first page, were the black-lettered words:

WOW!…NOW

Then underneath surrounded by a square, the letters: UR 4D

then underneath that: FRIENDSHIP

and then my name on top and his beneath, with two arrows on each side going in a clockwise direction, connecting the names. I had no idea what the acronyms meant, but I felt it would be rude to ask. Let him assume I knew.

On the second page was a simple image painted in three watercolors. I asked what it meant. He said he didn't know yet; it just came to him. I told him that I thought the four strokes of light blue represented the ocean, to which he agreed. I was very touched by his card. No one had ever made a home-made card for me before. Even though I didn't understand it, it moved me that he took the time and thought to produce this one-of-a-kind card just for me. In my head, I added another thing I liked about him on my list. I had to turn my head in the opposite direction to avoid him seeing me slightly tear up. We lay around for a long time, talking about each other's lives, and then he posed a question that I was not expecting.

"Are you having problems with your health?" I was taken by surprise, but I quickly recovered, and in a very composed manner responded, "Yes," and looked him directly in the eye.

"Are you in conflict with it?"

I told him that it has been a wake-up call, but I was dealing with it well, considering. He absorbed this information with a slight nod of the head. The questions stopped. He did not ask me anymore. I did not volunteer any more information.

After a brief silence of contemplation, his demeanor and attitude did not change towards me. It was a meaningful silence; I thought on ways to better handle this question in the future, as I was sure it would come up again. From gazing at his handsome features, his profile looked medieval. He reminded me of a young

Vincent Van Gogh. Breaking the ice, I asked if he was always this intense. With an air of confidence, he quickly said yes.

We watched an old Angie Dickerson movie called Dressed to Kill. I watched his animated disbelief at dated scenes from the movie. I liked the gentle way his left hand lay across his chest just below his nipple. They say that a man's fingers can resemble the shape of his penis. I liked his hands; they were clean, his nails neatly cut, and the tips of his fingers were bulbous. His hands represented such strength to me. They were firm and comforting, and in mine, they fit perfectly. These were the tools from which he made his living.

At one point during the course of this romantic foreplay, I reached over and sucked gently on his right thumb as he lay on his back, T-shirt pulled up above his nipples, which stood hard and alert. I looked at him as he softly moaned, his eyes closed. He looked so serene; I wanted his clothes off so I could admire all of him.

As our evening progressed, conversation became unnecessary. An unaccountable amount of time elapsed before I found myself waking up, my head on his chest, softly heaving with the life within it.

I gently raised myself up trying not to wake him. In the stillness of the night, I gazed on the man who was causing me to have such feelings. He looked so beautiful laying there. I scanned each part of him, touching him lightly with my fingertips from his head to his bare feet. He had nice feet: clear toenails that resembled the shape of his fingernails, with long toes and smooth soles. White people have such nice feet.

Lying on the floor below him were his ratty flip flops. They had somehow gotten intertwined with the laces of my yellow Timberland boots.

We are so different. What possessed us to like each other? I looked at the shoes in a different light, as if they were rings that fitted our feet instead of our fingers. I imagined his feet in those nasty flip flops next to mine at a cookout, in line at the movies, or facing each other at dinner.

He was still asleep. I counted the length of each breath until his rough hand grasped my head, playfully alerting me that he was awake. He took my face in his hands and looked into my eyes intently. Embarrassed and intrigued by such intimacy, I followed his lead, and said nothing to fuck up the moment. His eyes searched mine, as if looking for answers.

Then he gently retreated, removing the warmth of his hands from my cheeks and smiled. I wasn't sure if he'd gotten what he was looking for, but joined him with a silent smile. When he left that night, he turned around while at the top of the stairs and gave me a long, lingering look, smiled again, then ran down the stairs, humming to himself.

CHAPTER EIGHT

We did not speak again until I called him two nights later. I overwhelmed him with things I had been doing before I allowed him to speak. He'd been constantly in my thoughts, and when I finally had his ear, I took full advantage of it.

In my enthusiasm, I unintentionally mentioned that I was in therapy. It slipped out clearly before I could camouflage it with a cough or something. I had to be more on my guard with this man. I knew that the question from the other night was not closed and I had to be prepared for what he might throw my way. But to my surprise, he did not ask about it.

The next time I saw Aidan was on our first official date. I had gotten a couple of complimentary tickets to see a sex comedy on the Upper West Side. We arranged to meet early outside the theatre prior to the show. I was surprised when he showed up with Paloma, his dog, who was a cross between a pit bull and a Staffordshire. She was full of energy, very guarded towards me, and not very friendly. He told me she could be territorial, and that it was just her way of feeling me out to see if I was good for him.

He said this with a wicked smile, and then explained he had just walked her to do *her business,* and would I walk with them back to the car? He placed Paloma in the front passenger seat of his beat-up old car. I asked if she would be okay in there by herself, because the show was about ninety minutes. As we walked away from her whining, he assured me she would.

We sat up in the nosebleed seats of the small traditional

theatre. When the lights went down, he gently covered my hand with the warmth of his own on the armrest. During the show, I could see him looking at me out of the corner of my eye. One time, I had the courage to return his gaze, which quickly turned to embarrassment as he pouted his lips into an exaggerated silent kiss. I looked back towards the stage, self-conscious of whether the couple behind me had seen the gesture.

"Did I make you uncomfortable?" he whispered.

"No."

"Liar."

I sulked. His eyes smiled. If they could laugh, they probably would. He was taking advantage of my naiveté. He then whispered, "You look so good in the dark, I want to…" and his words faded off intentionally, so I wouldn't hear them. I didn't know if to take this as an insult or a compliment. What the hell did he mean about looking good in the dark? Was he saying I didn't in the light? I didn't know where the hell he was going with those words. I decided to leave it alone, before I started analyzing every action or alleged racial cliché.

The show focused mostly on the bedroom of a young couple coming to terms with being married and trying to spice up their sex lives. We had a few laughs; however, it was clear that this show wouldn't head downtown to Broadway. Afterwards, we picked up Paloma and found an Italian restaurant with plastic red-checkered tablecloths.

At dinner—with Paloma pouting and demanding attention at our feet—we briefly dissected the play, then focused on each other.

"Calm down. I'll feed and walk you soon," Aidan chastised Paloma. "You drank all your juice. You can have mine," he said, reaching over and placing his hand over mine, clasped around my cup.

"Nah, I'm good."

"It's okay. I didn't like it anyway," he said, and poured his juice into my cup. "Your hands are so smooth, and your skin is like milk chocolate."

I laughed, not sure I liked being compared to a piece of chocolate, but understanding his intent.

"It feels so good against mine," he continued. "Makes me wonder how it would be to hold you naked."

His words and the way he said it made me hot. The mischief in his eyes compelled me to return the feeling. Looking away for a moment, he rolled spaghetti on his fork and leaned over, gently coaching it into my unsuspecting mouth. I sucked up the last strand of spaghetti as his hand softly stroked my goatee. I looked around, embarrassed to see if anyone was looking, but he tugged on my goatee to face him again.

"No one cares around here, Isaiah," he said.

We finished our meal, absorbed in each other, oblivious of who else was around. After dinner, he drove me home. Paloma refused to sit in the back seat, so I had to. Three was a crowd, and this dog was getting on my nerves. Crossing the Brooklyn Bridge with outside traffic and a rushing train strained conversation, especially having to shout above that—not to mention the few disapproving looks Paloma would shoot me.

I invited him up for a night cap. He invited Paloma, which pissed me off. I kept thinking of the dog hair I'd have to sweep up afterwards. And god forbid he let that dog on my sofa. *You know how white people do*...and I caught myself. That was a racist thought. Funny; ordinarily I wouldn't have even considered that racist prior to meeting Aidan; I would have considered it fact.

We sat in the living room, sipping on two big mugs of green tea while he playfully tickled Paloma. I watched him under the soft lighting of my apartment; he looked Hispanic again. This man was a chameleon who changed under different light. For some reason, he looked different tonight; more mature and wiser than before. When he looked up, his eyes began to scan me, slowly lowering in descent.

At the moment, my desire for him was very strong. Something special was happening; we were communicating without words again. I felt a little warm, my heartbeat pounding in my head. I had to stop this urge, because it was too soon, yet I wanted him.

I wanted him now. I wanted him in my bed. Without thinking, I interrupted our non-verbal conversation.

"Aidan, I have something to tell you."

He did not respond, but waited on me to continue. I said a silent prayer, sipped a little tea to lubricate my mouth, which had suddenly become very dry, and said, "I am HIV positive."

I waited for an explosive reaction as I keenly looked at him. There was none. He gave me nothing to work with. He just sat there, waiting. Even Paloma was quiet, and looking at me expectantly.

"I've had this for the last ten years. For the most part, I've been healthy until recently. Earlier this year, I caught an opportunistic infection, and was hospitalized and put on medication. I am now on several of the AIDS cocktails."

Still, he said nothing. He had a vacant look on his face that I wanted to slap away. *Show something, whether it is anger, remorse, or compassion. Show me something.*

I went on to explain that I'd been dealing with it quite well. Sometimes I allowed myself to feel like a victim, sometimes I experienced great fear. Not so much so of death, but having to suffer to get there—and looking like shit in the process.

I told him that prayer and a new opening in my spiritual beliefs have been my saving grace, along with a change of diet and constant exercise which had kept me well until this recent illness, which I believed was brought on by stress.

The good news was that according to three psychics I'd seen over the past few years, I would live into old age. They didn't see me dying of this virus. This gave me hope, and had brought me through the last decade. Of course, I knew there were no guarantees, because if I didn't take care of myself, there were consequences—as I'd just experienced with this last illness. Prior to that, I had already proved their theory, so that kept me positive and didn't allow me to dwell on it.

I stopped talking and waited for him to speak. I had said too much, as usual. This was the one time that I should have said less.

It took him a few moments to collect his thoughts. "I know, but it sounds like you have it under control. Living in the now is a bitch! Life is a bitch." He chuckled. "Control is hard. Difficult. Things run the other way for me. Difficult; very, very difficult. It makes me so sad, sometimes angry."

I didn't know what the hell he was talking about. But I let him go on, hoping to make sense of the nonsense I was hearing.

"They say, get your head together and it's going to be okay. She promised me that. I'm waiting for that truth. Still waiting. It must be another lie."

"Who is she? Who are you talking about?" I asked.

"My therapist," he said simply without looking at me.

"You're seeing a therapist?"

"Yes."

I didn't know what to say next. I had just made a significant disclosure to him, and all I got was a mess of words and his issue.

"She told me I wasn't ready."

"Ready for what?" I almost snapped at him.

"For you."

"Oh? And how do you feel?" I asked in the same tone.

"I told her I was."

I was still confused. There was no us' being mentioned. I wanted to know if we had a future together. I understood this was shocking news to tell anybody, so I didn't want to pull anything out of him that he wasn't willing to give.

"I have to go," he said suddenly. "I have a contract I have to work on tonight for a bid in the morning."

I was about to protest, but changed my mind. It was better that this man got out of my apartment–now.

He stood up to leave. I glared at him for a moment, speechless. I pulled myself out of my self-induced trance and handed him a box of After Eights chocolates and a card from England. The card had a dancer on it, and inside, I had simply written, "You've touched me," and at the bottom, both our names and two male Mars symbols next to it. I told him that it was a friendship card, and he should read it when he got home.

He hugged me warmly, and rubbed my upper and lower back with his hands, just like he knew I liked. I tightened my grip on him even more. I felt him release his and pull away. He kissed me quickly on my forehead and left. As he closed the door softly behind him, there was no looking back.

CHAPTER NINE

After he left, I sat on the sofa and watched TV. Jay Leno of "The Tonight Show" was making fun of some dumb, obscure actress. I was astounded, confused, and pissed off, trying to make sense of what had just happened, mentally playing back what clues I had given him, where had I gone wrong.

Then it hit me. There was nothing else I could have done except not tell him the truth and I didn't want to do that, because I felt that this was going somewhere.

This was not the reaction I'd expected from him. Somehow, I had convinced myself that he would be more tolerant of HIV. So many in our community were ignorant and hateful to those who had it, as if they were immune to it. Many of them practiced unsafe sex, thinking they were invincible somehow particularly the young guys. The 'cocktail' had allowed this disease to go dormant, lurking in the underbelly of my system. They thought they were safe, but it pounced unannounced, uninvited. It infected silently, revealing its consequences at a later time—to the surprise of its host, as it had been for me.

I eventually found my way into bed, but lay there wide awake, unable to sleep after many attempts. My skin felt warm, almost feverish. I got up to drink some juice to relieve the tightness in my stomach. A nauseous feeling overcame me. I grabbed an ice pack from the freezer, wrapped it in a hand towel, and pressed it to the back of my neck. I stood with my forehead resting on the refrigerator door and quietly prayed for guidance and help to release the pain growing in me.

After the nausea had subsided, I pulled out my journal and

tried to record my feelings, hoping to release the stress that consumed me.

Nothing came to me. It was like I had writer's block. I felt so much, but couldn't find the words to convey it. After many false starts, I gave up, ending back up in the bed with my face buried in the pillow, praying that this was all a dream.

A few hours later, when nothing seemed to help, I decided to call my best friend David, who was probably not up yet. I dialed his number anyway, and surprisingly, he picked up on the first ring.

"Helloooo," he said with an extended yawn.

"David."

"What time is it?"

"I don't know."

"Well, you woke me up. I was having this strange dream, and it was getting to the part where…"

"David. I need you to shut up and listen!"

"What! Look, boyfriend, you call me at whatever goddam time it is and then you tell me to shut up?"

"I really need to talk to you," I said.

"What's wrong? You don't sound good."

"It's Aidan."

"The white boy?"

"Yes. I just told him everything about my status. He acted weird. Talking about control, it being difficult, how sad and angry he was. Then he said he was in therapy. He said she told him he wasn't ready to see me. He said he knew. How did he know, David? I don't look sick, do I?

"No, you don't. Calm down. Give him some time to absorb this. It's a lot for anyone to take. It's good that he wasn't hostile. You didn't have sex with him, did you?"

"No. I told him before I thought it could happen."

"You have to give him time; that's all you can do right now. The ball is in his court. You did the right thing. I think he'll respect you for that. It is best to start on an honest footing. From what you say, he has a lot of integrity."

I really didn't want to hear that, but I knew he was right. After

I hung up, I went back to my journal and found I was able to express myself a little more freely. However, as I re-read what I had written, it didn't truly convey the pain I was feeling. I felt so alone and unworthy.

Eventually, I did get a few hours' sleep, but woke up early and called my therapist to find out if he could fit me in today for a session; it was an emergency. He sensed the gravity in my voice, and arranged to squeeze me in later that afternoon.

I settled onto the leather couch next to my therapist's desk. It was cold and detached from the rest of the warm furnishings of his office. I pulled the Navajo blanket covered in colorful, rich earth tones from the arm of the sofa and laid it out, so I wouldn't touch the leather. My therapist watched me, amused at what had become a habit when I visited him.

"How are we feeling today, Isaiah?"

"Like shit."

"You don't look good. What's going on?"

"You would, too, if you had to deal with this crap." Without apologizing, I started to explain the previous night—probably over-dramatizing for effect, which seemed to be working, based on the surprised look on his face. He scribbled notes as I spoke, which turned out to be questions.

"What did you feel about Aidan's response to revealing your status?"

"Hurt. Confused. I expected sympathy, I guess."

"And when you didn't get that—"

"I know. How did you feel?" I interrupted, mimicking his routine. "Confused. I thought he was, also. Nothing he said made sense."

"Did it make you angry?"

"In a way, now that I think about it. I might have been okay with him being angry for a while, which is to be expected. But I trusted he would understand. That's why I thought I could tell him."

"Be mindful that anger is not always expressed violently or through verbal abuse. It can be confined within, which can be very dangerous. Isaiah, you may have to give him time to process this. This can be perplexing for some people."

"I know."

"In the meantime, I want you to take care of you. Put your needs first."

"What do you think, Doc? Is that a normal response you hear from your clients when someone reveals their status?"

"They have been subjective and different. It seems like Aidan should have handled this a little better, considering all the years of therapy he's had, which makes me question his emotional stability. You need to know that having HIV doesn't make you bad, and you shouldn't let anyone make you feel that way."

Before our session ended, he wanted to know if I would be willing to tell my story to the support group.

I told him I would have to think about it. I wasn't sure I wanted to share with some of those jaded faggots. I asked him why I needed to tell them anything.

He said it could be good for me to express myself publicly; it was all part of the process of creating a whole new me.

I shook my head at this lame answer, declared, "Whatever," and left.

Five days later, Aidan finally returned my calls. I told him that I needed to talk to him in person about our last meeting. He confessed that his confused state was probably due to a recent change in medication. For a minute, I didn't know what he was talking about. Then it dawned on me: he was on meds for his mental health. I didn't realize it was that serious. I decided not to question him about it at this time.

The following night Aidan returned holding a bottle of white wine and a wide grin. He was wearing a short-sleeve checkered shirt, tan cargo pants, and the same scruffy flip flop sandals I'd quickly come to dislike. I hadn't told him I didn't drink yet; instead, I took the bottle and put it in the refrigerator. Unexpectedly, his arms wrapped around me from behind pinning me to the refrigerator. The warmth of his body trapped mine. He gently kissed the back of my neck and slowly licked my ear, which tickled and made me shudder.

"What's wrong?" he asked.

"It tickled."

"Is that your weak spot?"

"Yes."

"I hardly know you and I've already found a vulnerable spot to have my way with you."

"What do you mean by that?" I said, winking.

"You'll see." He smiled devilishly, holding my hand and leading me to the sofa.

"What are we watching tonight?"

"I don't know yet. What do you feel in the mood for?"

"How about an old black and white movie with campy one-liners?"

"Bette Davis coming up."

He laughed approvingly as I searched for Bette. Gently he massaged my shoulders and my back.

"Do you go to the gym often?" he asked.

"At least three times a week depending on my work schedule."

"I don't work out. My job keeps me active, but I do yoga to stay toned.

"That you are."

"Thank you. I'd get bored lifting weights."

"It's not for everyone. It requires discipline."

"That's for sure."

"You mentioned work. What do you do?"

"I'm a project manager for a small marketing firm."

"Do you like it?"

"Yes, for the most part, even though my boss is tough. He relentlessly drives us to produce, stuffing us with donuts and caffeine to meet deadlines."

"You said 'for the most part.' Do you love your job?"

"No. Who does? It's a means to an end. Do you love yours?"

"I do. It took a lot of false starts before I found what feeds my spirit."

"And flipping houses does that?"

"Yep. I like working with my hands. Creating something that

lasts. Food doesn't do that." Then he asked, "Does your boss appreciate all your hard work?"

"I think so. I'm good at what I do."

"I'm glad I don't have a boss. I'm it. I've always resented bosses. I love the freedom and control. I try not to be like a boss, and almost treat my employees as equals. I find I get better results from them."

"How do you do that?"

"By listening to their input. Some of these guys have more experience than me in their field, and really know what they're doing."

"I'm glad that works for you. I'm not ready for that kind of responsibility and stress. Pay me and let me go home without having to think about this job till I set foot there the next morning."

Aidan looked at me in a peculiar way. I think he didn't like what I'd said. I changed the subject and went to get popcorn.

The rest of the evening we cuddled and laughed at the over-the-top Ms. Bette Davis until he said it was time for him to go home. There was no talk about my HIV status. I was hoping he'd bring it up, but he acted like I hadn't told him, which I found strange but quickly overlooked. He had come back, and that was all that mattered.

CHAPTER TEN

The next day I was surprised when Aidan called and asked me to lunch. We met at a city square near where I worked. We ordered tacos from a lunch truck parked nearby. While eating our tacos, we fed scraps to the pigeons that wanted to eat with us.

Aidan was wearing dark sunglasses which I politely asked him to take off. I'd gotten tired of talking to their glare. He blinked as his green eyes adjusted to the sunlight. Our conversation about our day competed with the background traffic, bustling shoppers, and a group of noisy barefoot teenagers throwing a frisbee.

A homeless man with blood-shot eyes and matted dreads approached us and silently held his hand out to share our tacos. I was about to dismiss him when Aidan handed him his taco with a couple of dollars. The man seemed indifferent to the gesture of kindness, and moved on to the lady on the next bench.

"I hate how this city ignores the mentally ill," Aidan said, looking sadly after the man.

"How do you know he's mentally ill?"

"Did you see his eyes? They were vacant, they had no life behind them."

"No, I didn't notice that. Guess I've gotten used to it, like most New Yorkers."

Aidan turned from watching the man and looked at me in disbelief.

"I notice. I can always tell. People don't notice because they don't want to care," he said curtly.

"Aidan, I didn't mean to sound uncaring but it's the reality of living in this city. We have to take it for granted, or it will drive you nuts."

I got another odd look from him.

"Not me. That's why I like the country, being in nature with animals. I have peace there."

I resumed eating my tacos. The moment felt awkward. I didn't know what to say next, because I thought I'd offended him somehow. My cellphone rang and saved me. It was a coworker telling me that my client had arrived early for my next appointment. I explained to Aidan I had to leave.

"Go take care of your business. I'm sorry, but I can be a radical prick at times. Are we good?" he asked.

"Yes, we are."

"Sounds good. I'll call you later"

I hurried back to work. When I had some down time, I thought about what happened in the park. I was touched by his compassion for the homeless, especially since the man had the added burden of being mentally ill. What seemed to trouble him the most was my indifferent attitude to it. I didn't see anything wrong with what I'd said. My statement was a common one New Yorkers would make.

His compassion moved me though and made me question how the city had hardened me to the plight of others. For the first time I realized I was cocooned in my own bubble of work, friends, my health, sex and men. I wondered if Aidan was my wake-up call? Was I ready for that?

He didn't call later. All night I waited for his call until I reluctantly fell asleep. The next day the same thing. Maybe he was waiting for me to call? I didn't want to give the impression I was pursuing him, which I had a tendency to do when I really like someone. I called him when I got home.

"Hey, what's up!" he said cheerfully.

"Just checking in. How are you?"

"I'm fine."

"What are you up to?"

"Babysitting"

"Babysitting!" I repeated with surprise. Oh god, don't tell me he has a kid.

"Yeah, my neighbors' kids. They're driving me crazy but we're having fun."

I could hear a cartoon playing on the TV and the squealing kids.

"How many kids?"

"Two."

"Sounds like a bunch of them."

"Believe me, these kids have so much energy, I don't know how Regina copes."

"How long are you babysitting tonight?"

"I'm not sure. It's usually a couple of hours before Regina and Jack get home."

"Oh! Okay, I was hoping to take you to dinner tonight."

"That's sweet," he joked mockingly. "And you're paying right?"

"Of course."

"Then you have a date, as long as you open the car door and pull back the seat for me at the restaurant," he continued to tease me.

"I get it, I wasn't trying to emasculate you."

"Isaiah, I'm kidding. Lighten up. How about you come here?"

"What now? And with the kids there?"

"Yeah, now."

"But their parents, what will they think when they see a stranger with their kids?"

"Regina and Jack are very cool. They trust me. They know I'd never put these little darlings in any kind of danger. I'll just tell them you're my new boyfriend."

I loved it when he said that. I hesitated; I'd hoped to be alone with him tonight.

"I'll text you the address."

There was a loud crash. One of the kids started to cry.

"Got to go. Eric, I told you not to pull on that..." and the phone disconnected.

After finding parking, I knocked on the door. Aidan opened it, a little girl with milky skin sat on his shoulders. Her tiny hands clasped around his head, feet dangling in front of his chest. Holding his hand by his side, was a chubby little boy with flushed cheeks and chocolate smeared around his mouth. Aidan looked like a dad. The kids could have been his own.

"Isaiah this is Tracy," he said, pointing at her with his free hand, "and this is Eric," who was now swinging on his other arm. "Say hello, kids."

"Hello, Isaiah!" they both said in a sing-song way.

"You brought any candy?" Eric asked, eyeing my pockets.

"No more candy for you, Eric. Let's go wipe that mouth."

I stepped into the apartment closing the door behind me. It was what you'd expect with two young kids. Disorganized chaos, like an earthquake had shook it. Dirty dishes in the sink and dining table, half-eaten pizzas, toys on every surface and kids' dirty clothing in piles on the carpet.

Tracy ran back into the room and stared at me curiously. Eric screamed with resistance as Aidan wiped his mouth. I started to think that me coming here was not such a great idea. About two hours later that opinion had changed. The kids were finally in bed after much coercing. Aidan and I lay spread out on the sofa, mentally exhausted.

"That Eric is a little devil. He cheats," I said laughing.

"I know, I should have warned you."

"Why didn't you?"

"I wanted to find out if it was only me he did it to."

"Well now you know. I must admit, this was a lot of fun, though."

"It was, wasn't it? I like to escape into their world to decompress from the stresses of mine."

"You don't appear to have stress to me. You're always so laid back and in control."

"Believe me, I have my moments."

We fell into silence of contemplation. I didn't know what he was thinking, but I was wondering what he was like when stressed out or even angry. I liked to see all sides of people, not just what they wanted to present to the world.

"Isaiah."

"Yes, Aidan?"

"I really like how you told that bedtime story to Tracy. You had her totally believing that hooey mess those children's book writers came up with."

"It's a classic tale. Girl meets boy, but she's a princess and he a commoner. She gets kidnapped by the wicked witch, he finds her and saves the day, and they live happily ever after. The end."

"You were really good. I was watching you. You're good at this. Ever thought of being a father someday?"

"Hell nah!" I responded.

"I do. It's something I want someday, when I'm in a committed relationship again."

Just then, we heard the front door being opened. Regina and Jack were home.

That weekend Aidan invited me to a jazz concert in honor of the late Charlie Parker in Thompson Square Park the following day, and to meet his best friend, James. I arrived an hour late with my best friend, David.

The park was more crowded than I had anticipated, filled with all kinds of jazz buffs and local residents of the East Village. The park filled with noises of excitement and anticipation from those expecting a good concert and those that had just come to crowd watch. The mixed smells of incense, beer, and weed assaulted my nostrils. I was worried about finding Aidan amongst all these people. David seemed more concerned about moving forward to check out the musicians.

I turned to protest, but the presence of Aidan stopped me. He had suddenly materialized from behind a pallid-skinned punk rock woman with many striking tattoos. He stared at me fondly, Paloma on a leash at his side. I introduced him to David. Paloma barked. She snuggled up to David as he petted and complimented her. She recoiled from me when I tried to do the same—was this dog trying to tell me something?

After brief chatter, David left us to get closer to a jazz quartet that had just started to jam. Aidan, Paloma, and I stood by a park fence watching the crowd and each other. I was a little hesitant towards him, not knowing how he was feeling towards me. So far, he had been cordial, but I needed more than that to feel relaxed with him.

"Stop looking so worried. All will be okay. I want you to enjoy yourself." And then he smiled like he was reading my mind. His smile disarmed all my doubts. It told me to proceed, no matter the consequences. *I don't think he's going to desert me, not like the others.* I smiled back, but it was no ordinary smile—wide, bright, and encouraging, but meant to disarm him into submission. I wanted him to know that he wasn't the only one with charm.

Paloma was very popular with passersby. There were a lot of mixed couples in the crowd, both gay and straight, which made me feel more comfortable with him. A lot of artists and particularly dancers he knew would stop by, standing in second position as if about to do a plié, graceful hands adding flourishes to what they were saying. I basked in his presence, revelling; an occasional touch of the shoulder, a whisper in the ear when the music got loud, an introduction to a friend that would afford him the opportunity to throw his arm around me like we had been boyhood friends.

"Hold that pose." David had returned, holding a camera ready to snap a picture of us. "Smile!"

We both gave the cheesiest smiles we could as Aidan's arm dropped wrapping around my waist, pulling me closer to him.

"That's going to be a lovely picture. You make a nice couple," David said, smiling and giving me a wink.

I didn't want Aidan to remove his arm from my waist. I wanted it to stay there for as long as we were in the park—but he removed it after the picture was taken.

After an hour, David reminded me that we had an eight o'clock show to catch an off-Broadway musical in the West Village. We all agreed to meet after the show at a Chinese restaurant down the street from the theatre.

Full of unclear symbolism and third-rate singers, the show was awful! As the musical progressed, some audience members began to leave. David and I were stuck in the middle of a full row near the front, so close that during an up-tempo number, I could have sworn one of the twirling singers spat at me. As the musical progressed, it lost even more focus and became boring. David fell asleep several times, only waking up when I nudged him from snoring.

CHAPTER ELEVEN

Aidan and his best friend James were already seated in the middle of the crowded restaurant patio when we arrived. James was a psychotherapist originally from the south. He was a touch effeminate, with red hair and wide hips, and reminded me of the actor Phillip Seymour Hoffman. I reached out to shake his hand, but he moved a chair so I could sit. Then he moved to a chair opposite me, presumably to scrutinize me. He looked at me in an odd manner—if I were to guess, it was almost as if he couldn't believe it. I assumed that Aidan had already told him what color I was, and I was sure it wasn't his first time meeting a black date of Aidan's.

After initial ice breakers, the conversation struck up speed, and flowed easily, with lots of laughter, because James was very funny. However, he took full advantage of every moment he got to slyly interrogate me. I knew what he was doing. Now I had him and Paloma to deal with.

"Aidan tells me that you enjoy art."

"Yes, I do."

"What is your favorite period?"

"My taste is simple, I'm afraid, because it is still all relatively new to me. I do like Pop and Afro-centric art."

"Oh really? I tend to like baroque, impressionism, and a little bit of cubism. I would have taken you to be a cubism man."

"I'm not sure what kind of art that is?"

"Oh yes, you did say you were a novice in these things. Picasso was one of the pioneers in cubism. More bread?"

"Stop being a pompous bore, James," Aidan interrupted.

"The Charlie Parker concert earlier was wonderful," David piped in cheerfully. I looked at him with relief.

"I don't care for Modern Jazz. I just don't understand it. All that wailing and scatting, and instruments making noise. Give me Lena Horne and an orchestra, good brandy, and I'm in heaven," James said, taking a big gulp of his margarita.

David leaned over to me as the waiter brought our appetizers. "This bitch is crazy. She has a negative opinion on everything."

I smothered a smile. I knew what he was up to, but decided to be on my best behavior for Aidan's sake.

Two margaritas later, James became a little loose at the mouth.

"Where is our food?" declared James, who was slowly turning into a southern belle. "The help here is so slow."

David and I looked at each other. Aidan saw this. Looking a little embarrassed, he quickly said, "James, the restaurant is full. They're busy. Be patient?"

"No dear, I can't."

"Eat some more bread."

"And have it go straight to my hips…no, no dear."

"So how was the play?" Aidan asked.

"It sucked," David said.

"I did some of that last night," James intervened. "Sucking, I mean. Nice little boy from Minnesota or Missourah or one of them Midwest states. He was a lovely mouthful."

And he started to laugh, or should I say, it was more of a giggle. He was certainly being inappropriate. It was clear when we were introduced that he'd already had a few on an empty stomach, but now his language was heading for the gutter. I wondered why Aidan had such a queen as a best friend.

"Okay, James, that's enough TMI," Aidan scolded him.

"Why darling, I'm sure everyone present has sucked a dick or two. We're all big boys…especially you two," he said, and indicated David's and my crotch with his head.

"Okay, James. I think you've had enough," Aidan chided him again.

"I never get enough. I have an insatiable appetite, haven't you heard?"

"Yes, I know."

Aidan tried to take James's drink away, but he wouldn't let him. They struggled playfully, but James was not letting go of that cocktail. Seeing that it was causing attention from other diners, Aidan gave up.

"Okay, James. Promise you'll behave."

"I will, baby. Promise. So, you are his new beau?" James said, pointing a plump finger at me. "You look like all the others."

"Others? What do you mean by that?" I asked. He was beginning to tick me off.

"Your features, dear. Dark and lovely negroid features...the nose, the hair, the lips, etcetera. It's uncanny how much you look like the two boyfriends before you."

"Okay, James, that's enough," Aidan said sternly.

"That's what I said to the Missourah boy last night." He giggled. "Yes, dear. Terrence was a sweetheart. I liked him. Gone too soon. Pity."

David and I watched Aidan. He'd become even more agitated, and slightly red in the face. He'd been unsuccessful at silencing his friend, and looked like he was about to shut him up when I jumped in.

"And the other one. What was he like?"

"Ah, Marcel!" James said in a poor imitation of a French accent. "Didn't know him. Just heard some things. Questionable past."

"Enough, James!"

"Sorry, sweetie. I'll shut up now. Waiter where's our food!" He wailed.

Finally, steaming hot platters of stir-fried vegetables, chow mein, shrimp with broccoli, moo goo gai pan, and crabmeat lo mein arrived. Aidan looked relieved. James devoured the spring rolls, dipping them into a hot sauce that made him scream for water. The food had his attention now. Small talk was between mouthfuls but a lot tamer than before. Aidan tried to recover from his friend's 'oversharing' with trite conversation, but it was clear that he wasn't happy. *I would love to hear the conversation those two have after we leave them.*

I had hoped to spend a little time alone with Aidan after

dinner, but it was clear that James was in no condition to go home alone. David and I saw them off in a cab, and walked towards the subway.

"That queen was a hoot." David started to laugh. "And what was all that about his previous boyfriends? He put Aidan's business in the street. *No offense, dear,*" he said, imitating James, and indicating that I wasn't the street.

"I know. Aidan got really riled up about it, especially when he mentioned Marcel."

"And what was all that 'questionable past' about?" David asked, looking to me for an answer.

"The hell if I know. But I want to find out about both of them."

The following day I called Aidan to thank him for the wonderful time David and I had, in spite of James. He said he was in the midst of cleaning his loft, clearing out accumulated junk picked up on the streets over the years, but was having a hard time parting with some of it. I made small talk with him, hoping at some point he would invite me on a date—alone this time. But he didn't, so I made an excuse to get off the phone, a little embarrassed because I was so obvious, and he didn't take the bait.

I didn't hear from him for several days. Many times, I picked up the phone to call, but couldn't. I was beginning to appear desperate, and that did not sit well with me. I was giving up hope of ever hearing from him again when the phone rang one night. He said he had something on his mind that he wished to express, and eventually, out of casual conversation, I heard what I suspected.

"I know you've thought my behavior odd lately?"

"No, not really. No odder than usual," I joked.

He didn't laugh with me. "My medication has changed...I mean, I'm adjusting to the side effects. I take it for depression." I listened in stunned silence. "Depression seems to be hereditary in my family—on my father's side. I always thought I was moody. My father knew the real reason, but kept it from me, hoping not to encourage me to think in that direction. I grew up with mood swings, isolating myself, and sometimes anger would manifest.

So, I escaped to Paris. It was the most freeing thing I could have done. In Paris, I found me, the real me. I worked in a restaurant, and shared a cramped apartment with another American student. It was probably one of the happiest times in my life. It was in Paris that I first fell in love with a man named Marcel. He was 'out,' but in a masculine way. I didn't think back then that such people existed. I always thought that 'out' meant being a queen. I struggled not to love him, but couldn't help myself. Marcel was fascinating and irresistible."

"Marcel was French?" I asked, surprised to hear that he had a white boyfriend.

"Yes, but he was of Rwandan heritage."

"Oh."

"His parents were refugees from Rwanda that fled their country to escape persecution. His parents, of course, disapproved of his lifestyle, especially as he was brought up in the Muslim faith. I learned from him what holding all that pain inside for so long can do. He has no relationship with his parents now." Aidan got quiet over the phone for too long a period.

"Are you okay?" I asked.

"I can't talk about him anymore. It's too painful."

"I understand." I really didn't, but what does one say under these circumstances? I wanted to hear more about the mysterious Marcel and his 'assumed' disappearance from Aidan's life. But the finality in his tone told me I would have to learn that story another day. He became quiet again.

He had been on a roll, and I didn't want him to stop sharing who he was now, so I asked, "What happened after Paris?"

"I came home. I had this stupid conviction that I needed to come out to my parents, thinking they could handle it because they probably already knew. But I was wrong. It didn't go so well. My father called me a 'punk' and stormed out of the house. My mother fell apart and just cried non-stop. He didn't return for two days, and then I was politely asked to leave."

"Where did you go?"

"New York." We both started to laugh. It was so cliché. The Frank Sinatra anthem came to mind.

"What happened here?"

"I worked in a restaurant, in the kitchen, and worked my way up to pastry chef."

"You can bake?"

"I make a mean German chocolate cake."

"Maybe I can taste it one day. I'll tell you if it's any good," I teased.

"Terrence always liked it."

"Terrence? Was he your last lover?"

"Yes."

"Were you in love with him, too?"

"Yes, very much."

"So, what happened? Why aren't you with him now?"

"He died."

"Oh, I'm so sorry. What did he die of?"

"AIDS." He said it so casually.

I froze.

"He's another one I do not want to talk about." He said that like a command. Then he paused for a long time, as if he was considering something. He must have relented, because he continued to talk about Terrence again without my encouragement.

"I fell into a deep depression. I started to drink beer and cheap wine, and eventually graduated to hard liquor. Then I met someone at a party in the East Village who introduced me to mind-altering drugs. That seemed to make the pain and depression disappear for a while. But it returned, and I did more drugs. Then I couldn't handle my days without the drugs. I knew I had a problem. I even tried AA for a bit, but the depression wouldn't go away.

"Then, one night after getting high with that same friend, I was on my way home on my bike, and a truck hit me on Spring St. I went through his windscreen. Two weeks later, I woke up from a coma in the hospital. It took almost eight months of rehab to recuperate, because I had developed some neurological problems. But my parents took care of me like I had never left, as if I was the same old me. But I'd changed. Something traumatic like that changes you. Now do you see why I do the meds and need therapy?"

"Yes." I said weakly, forced into submission of sadness and empathy.

I had listened in silence, holding back comment unable to imagine the trauma of all those experiences. The pain I heard in his voice was like he was reliving it. I wanted to reach out and hug him, hold him close to me, as if that would take away the pain. I told him I needed to see him; I missed talking to him face-to-face.

There was silence on the other end of the phone. Then I heard what sounded like a sigh before he responded. He invited me to come to his apartment later on that night. He gave me directions, then hung up the phone.

CHAPTER TWELVE

Two hours later, I was in the car, driving on Bedford Avenue through a Hasidic neighborhood of Williamsburg. All these years in New York, and I had never been to this part of the city. Jews in black hats, long beards and ankle-length black coats scurried swiftly on the streets. Some darted into rows of red brick attached brownstones. Very little light seemed to come from any of them—most of the neighborhood was already asleep.

Aidan lived in a loft apartment on the third floor of a dilapidated building. He came down to let me in through these huge steel doors, and I followed him up a dimly-lit pee-scented stairwell to his floor.

I walked into a brightly lit artist's space. My first impression was of orderly chaos. Many uneven bookshelves lined the walls, filled with mostly books about art and classic fiction. There was a lot of cabinet space, some of which were open and filled with artists' materials. Canvas paintings of various sizes were strewn around the room, half-hidden in corners or out-of-the-way places.

There was a lot of old antique furniture, some of which was in poor states of disrepair. The kitchen appeared cleaner than I had expected. Lots of brass pots and pans hung over the white Formica countertop and bare cement floor. There was a small bathtub on a raised platform in the bathroom, and his unmade bed seemed to rise out of an alcove in the living room. Paloma stood in the middle of the kitchen, tail wagging furiously, and quite leery of me. She was her usual selfish self, always demanding attention and getting it.

A particular photograph prominently displayed on top of an antique bureau caught my eye. I lifted it up to inspect it. Aidan was in the middle, with his arms around the shoulders of two men; one older white man with a salt-and-pepper beard, and a young black man that looked like me. He could have been easily mistaken for me, except that he didn't have glasses. My whole body stiffened. I was suddenly aware that Aidan stood right behind me.

"That was my lover and my best friend. They both died from AIDS."

I was so shocked at these few words that I didn't know what to say. I was also pissed off that the lover looked like me. What the fuck was Aidan up to? I already knew how Terrence died. What I didn't know was that he was the spitting image of me. I felt like the butt of a sick joke.

I excused myself to the bathroom, feeling like I wanted to throw up. I cupped both hands with cold water and splashed the cool liquid onto my face over and over again. I looked at my tired face in the mirror. I really hadn't paid much attention before, but I hadn't slept well in weeks. There were dark circles below my eyes, and I looked worn out. My face no longer looked vibrant. Stress had sucked it out of me.

I looked like shit.

"Are you okay?" he said from outside the bathroom door.

"Yeah, I'm fine."

"You looked ill for a minute."

"It's nothing. Just a little indigestion from something I ate earlier," I lied.

My thoughts rushed back to the situation at hand as I wiped my face with sheets of one-ply toilet paper. I was the rebound guy, a substitute for his dead lover. I just didn't know it.

What kind of sick mind am I dealing with? This fucker is truly crazy. He doesn't need therapy; he needs to be committed.

I flicked damp wads of toilet paper lint off my face, put on my glasses, and rushed out of the bathroom with the intention of getting out of this fucking loft.

I was stopped dead in my tracks by the presence of Aidan, who stood in the middle of the kitchen floor under a low-hanging light above his head like a halo. He looked ethereal, angelic yet childlike. He looked at me with those intense eyes, and I conceded. I couldn't move, transfixed by this image of him. All I could think of was that this was fucking surreal.

"You know, don't you?" he said in a resigned manner.

I nodded.

"That's why I ran the other way when I first saw you in the park. I thought I'd seen a ghost. You scared me, but I knew you weren't a ghost. I had to find out why the universe had destined us to meet. That's why I came back to find you."

Now I really wanted to run, but I couldn't. My feet just wouldn't carry me out of there. For a moment, I had a vision of him pulling one of those large kitchen knives and plunging it into me for being an imposter, for not being the real thing, for not being Terrence. It didn't seem so far-fetched. This motherfucker was certifiable.

He continued, "But then I got to know you, and I realized you weren't him. You didn't think like him, you didn't talk like him; you didn't crinkle your nose when something puzzled you, like him. You were not him, and I woke up."

He seemed very far away, yet so near. He had this celestial look on his face, like if Terrence was in the room and he was talking to him. His face was filled with love, and I knew now that it wasn't directed at me.

A long silence followed. We both cradled our thoughts—he, with his beloved Terrence, me, blaming myself for falling in love with a man that was not emotionally available.

He offered to make some tea. I sat and watched him as he prepared it, how comfortably he moved in his own space. Our conversation was labored, and continued to be separated by awkward silences. This time, I sensed we didn't know what to say to each other. We no longer seemed to have anything in common.

He served me the tea in a large white mug with a chip on the rim. I sipped the hot tea slowly, trying not to get burned and cut at the same time. He ate the remains of a leftover salad, and didn't offer me any. Then it was time to walk the dog. In a little neighborhood park two blocks away, we sat on a bench and watched Paloma play with her red ball.

It was at this point he resumed our previous conversation, like it had just taken place. I was beginning to wonder if he had taken his medication today. I listened to the content of what he was saying. Much of it was of his remembrance of Terrence and how they paid tribute to their love by exchanging special gifts—which he indicated by looking at the gold band on his finger. The rest of it, I tuned out, because I didn't care. It was when he started talking about me that my attention returned.

He said that he found me judgmental. He noticed it in the beginning, and thought it would go away, but it didn't. I was always telling him how he should be. I put it in the form of a suggestion, but he saw through the disguise, and took it for what it was; straight-up criticism. He said it angered him. It reminded him of what living at home with his parents was like.

I was very surprised and shocked to hear this, because I always thought my advice was well-delivered and given with the best intent. He always accepted it with quiet gratitude, but no response. I thought it was appreciated.

Then I realized something. I was about to get angry at this confrontation-of-sorts, and it hit me. Maybe he was right. I needed to look at this behavior. I decided not to respond and accept it like he did—with quiet gratitude.

An hour later, I left Aidan. We hugged several times—each time initiated by me. They were strong bear hugs that lacked the passion or the desire to explore further, as they once had. They were hugs of farewell.

When I got home, I took a long shower. The water coasted across my body as I stood motionless, consumed with my thoughts, which seemed to come in flashbacks. I remembered moments of tenderness, confusion, rage, and visions of a future together that was never to be.

Then the tears came, and they wouldn't stop. The pain in my gut intensified. What seemed like hours later, I became aware of still being naked with a towel wrapped around my waist, sitting on the closed toilet seat, the shower water still running—now cold. I didn't know how long I had been sitting there. All I knew was that, like the water, I was cold.

CHAPTER THIRTEEN

Many weeks passed, but that fateful night refused to leave my head. Thanksgiving came and went. I'd refused invitations to dinner and stayed at home in bed, binge-watching TV.

On my way to work, I thought about him in line at the bank, I thought about him, even taking a shit—I really thought about him. I rationalized that in defecating, I was releasing him from my system, letting go of the anger and the feeling of being used and abandoned. However, my affirmations to let him go and focus on me didn't work; neither did prayer.

Then, one day, I realized that I was trying too hard to forget him, and that in doing so, I was keeping the hurt alive. My feelings for him were not lessening, but strengthening, even though conflicted with anger and love. I feared that word, love. It was what I wanted to experience most in my life, and I was getting it—the only problem was the man was not around to share it.

One night, I was driving home with the radio off. Aidan was on my mind. I didn't know how it happened, but I passed my stop and continued down Atlantic Avenue, past desolate warehouses and poorly lit streets, until I saw Hasidic men in black earnestly heading home. I parked the car behind another, across the street from the park where he walked Paloma, and waited.

I had no idea what I was doing, except that I felt compelled to be there and to allow whatever was to be. Only two residents were in the park: a white woman with a green scarf around her head and a loose grey tracksuit, waiting impatiently for her Labrador to poop.

The other person was a Middle Eastern-looking gentleman speaking Arabic loudly on his cell phone. She glared at him, probably disturbed by the harsh tone of his voice, while she drew on the last remnant of her cigarette. They did not appear to know each other. I wondered if they knew Aidan. They had to; if not by name, then by sight. It's interesting how New Yorkers do not know or care to know about their neighbors. In many ways, people in this city are selfish. Too many times have I witnessed people stepping over bodies asleep or drunk on the streets, not caring if the person was even alive.

I didn't have to wait long before Paloma ran into the park, unleashed and barking at the Labrador. They sniffed each other and started to play. I thought, *we humans could learn a lot from dogs.* Aidan ran into view, calling out to Paloma, swinging her leash. He was smiling and appeared to be happy.

But he was not alone. A few steps behind him was an attractive, dark-skinned man, trying to keep up. Aidan waved at the woman in the green scarf. She responded with a tired wave of her right hand. He went over to a bench in the park and sat down, with his friend joining him. Paloma continued to romp with the Labrador. The black man crossed his legs and leaned back on the bench, pulling his hoodie over his head, and turned to face Aidan, who seemed to be explaining something.

Aidan lit a cigarette. *That's odd, I didn't know he smoked.* They both laughed at something amusing. Then he handed the cigarette to the man. *Wait a minute.* That was no cigarette—it was a joint. *I didn't know he did that, either.* After a while. they laughed out loud and smiled more—I could see the dimple in Aidan's cleft chin when he threw his head back. The conversation on Aidan's part became more animated, while the man still reclined back on the bench, his legs apart and his hands in the hoodie pockets, the oversized hood hiding all but the tip of his nose and lips.

Aidan said something to him, and then touched his thigh. I could have sworn he squeezed it and held it for a moment, while looking to see if anyone caught it.

I was devastated. I had already been replaced. This was no casual friend; there was more going on here.

I wanted to start the car and get the hell out, but I didn't want to alert them to my presence, because Aidan knew my car. I watched as Aidan leaned back inches from the man's face saying something that seemed to be intimate, causing them both to stare at each other—unaware of the two people in the park. Paloma ran between Aidan's legs, interrupting this intimate moment. Having tired of the Labrador, who finally did his business, that bitch knew how to upstage a moment. Aidan's friend reached over and playfully rubbed Paloma's belly. It surprised me that she allowed this. I could never get away with that.

The Labrador and owner exited the park, dumping the dog's plastic bag excrement in the garbage. I hadn't noticed that the man on the cellphone had left. Aidan and his friend were now in the park alone. Aidan's hand found its way to the man's thigh again, and stayed.

The conversation had grown more intimate and more serious, to the point that even Paloma behaved and sat quietly panting. The man spoke for a long time as Aidan listened without the cheerfulness of before, but with something so pressing that even Aidan was speechless. Then, in unison, they got up to leave. Aidan's arm around his shoulder and then slipping to rub him in the middle of his back, like he used to do to me.

I must have sat in my car for a good half hour, breaking down what I had just witnessed. The man was really attractive, maybe even handsome. He was very dark-skinned, with a broad forehead and large lips. His baggy clothing didn't hide the hint of a great body beneath. He was masculine, and walked elegantly at the same time, with a little bit of swag thrown in.

I had been replaced. There was no mourning period for me, like I did for him. I had not looked at another man since our breakup, even for mere lust—a breakup that was not even official.

We hadn't called each other since that night. We just knew it was over. But since then, my feelings had recanted. I wanted him, even more than when I was with him. Over a joint, I had daydreamed about how to get him back, how to win his love. How to let him know that I had changed and was addressing my faultfinding with my therapist. Now I had some serious competition. How the fuck was I going to compete with that?

For two days, I lay in bed, depressed and feeling sorry for myself, the helpless victim with a broken heart. I went on his AOL social media account to see what he was up to currently, but he hadn't posted anything new. I drooled over the few pictures he had posted, mostly with Paloma.

I reread some of the texts he'd sent me. The romantic ones. The ones that just said, *thinking of you or, can't wait to see you later.* I even had a couple of voicemails he'd left that I kept renewing so that they wouldn't be deleted. These were not romantic, but they had his voice. I replayed them many times just to hear him speak and laugh. I looked at the home-made card he'd made for me, and reveled in the sentiment of which it was given. That one always made me sad.

I must have watched every damn soap opera that I could stomach and a bunch of chick flicks on the Lifetime TV channel. I was becoming adept at playing the victim. I analyzed my stalking observation to death. Who was the black stranger? How long had he known him? Had he told him about me? Had he asked him about his health status to avoid making the same mistake twice? All these questions traveled through my head, punching holes like a sewing machine, creating this tapestry of little pricks that reverberated through me.

I hadn't taken my meds in the past two days. I just didn't want to. I was supposed to take them every day for life. Missing doses could make them lose their effectiveness, and god knows there were few options left if I exhausted all of the limited protease inhibitors. The choice of antiviral drugs to treat HIV were few. There were always drugs being developed, but it took them years to get to human trials. When nothing no longer worked, many had died waiting. I knew of a few guys that went that route.

These thoughts of what I wasn't doing scared me. I made my way to the cabinet, where I kept my medications hidden behind tall cereal boxes. I slowly put them in my mouth, one at a time, followed by water. I left the nastiest for last: a big pill, which I could never pronounce the name of, flushing it with even more water. It almost made me choke several times. Now, wouldn't it be embarrassing if choking on a pill killed me before HIV? I always followed my meds with a probiotic pill. It stopped the drugs from depleting all the good bacteria in my system, balancing it out so I could digest my food and not have bad breath. Or *drug breath,* as David called it. I was surprised at how accustomed I'd grown to taking these daily pills for the rest of my life. It had become routine, just like eating.

David was avoiding my calls. He was always busy. I knew he'd grown tired of my whining and detailed examinations of what had taken place between Aidan and me. I wanted to tell him about the new dark stranger. I wanted his advice on who he might be and what I should do. Then I had to remind myself, *you are no longer with him. Get over it.*

I had grown tired of the anger on a new reality show I was watching. I took the remote and started switching the channels to something more palatable. Then something caught my eye, and made me return to the previous station I had just clicked past. It was the BBC channel.

They were doing an exposé on a terrorist group. They showed a lineup of faces wrapped in turbans and hidden by long beards. The one face that made me return to this station was not like the others. His features were not hidden by hair or cloth.

His face was raw and exposed. A dark, even skin tone gleamed. A broad nose, but structured to a point at the tip. Very generous lips parted to reveal a splash of white teeth that gleamed as much as his skin. This was not the normal picture of a terrorist. It was not taken with a smirk or a moving mouth spewing out heated propaganda. This young man was striking and familiar. I knew that face. It didn't take me long before my memory confirmed who I thought it might be—yet I still wasn't sure.

The BBC newscaster moved onto another story. I waited fifteen minutes for them to repeat the same story. They didn't. The news ended and moved onto a documentary. The image of the guy was still in my head. I wanted to know more. I flipped to other news channels to see if the story was being repeated there.

After three of them, I gave up and fired up my dormant computer. I went to the BBC website and did a search. Success was instant. The heading read, *Lone Wolf Terrorist Attack Imminent.* I scrolled down and read the story which was very detailed, with British vocabulary like 'queue' for a line or 'lorry' for a truck. It gave a brief history of each of the six terrorists pictured.

The dark stranger's bio was next to the last. His first name made me stiffen: Marcel Bahati. I barely noticed his last name. The first name was enough. I quickly read the short paragraph of his history. He was either a member or sympathizer of an Al-Qaeda affiliated group. He was second-generation French. Had been arrested multiple times in protests. He was known to recruit and possibly train young converts. He had disappeared, and was thought to have left France. He was wanted for questioning due to the killing of a French soldier. His prints were found at the scene. The article didn't give more details, as this was an ongoing investigation.

Impulsively, I printed his picture. I had no idea why or what I was going to do with it, but I did. The color copy of his striking face stared back at me from my desk. My desk lamp illuminated the skin and the half smile. He was smiling at me—a sly smile, devilish. His eyes, though bright, contained a dark undertone that lay beneath. I didn't know if it was in my own imagination, but as my evening progressed, every time I returned to look at that picture, that darkness in the eyes still remained.

I could no longer focus on the TV. While eating a bowl of pasta and vegetables sprinkled with seasoned chicken, it came to me. I got dressed and jumped in my car–Marcel's picture safely enclosed in a manila envelope on the front passenger seat.

CHAPTER FOURTEEN

I crossed the Brooklyn Bridge into Manhattan. Traffic was mild, so I made good time to Williamsburg—close enough to when I suspected Aidan would walk that bitch Paloma. It took me a while to parallel-park a safe but close enough distance away, where my car wouldn't be recognized. Next to the manila envelope was my camera. I prepared it to shoot. I settled down, listened to a talk show on radio station WBLS, and waited.

I waited forty-five minutes before I saw Paloma bounding around the corner unleashed. Why does he release his dog like that before reaching the Park? Isn't that dangerous? Aidan was fairly close behind, but alone, with headphones in his ears. His head moved rhythmically to whatever he was listening to—probably something like Steely Dan. He loved jazz-rock even though that band was around before he was born.

He threw Paloma's red ball across the green, and drooling and panting energetically, she dutifully retrieved it. He did it again, and she rushed off. *If I were a dog, I wouldn't go. I would think it was humans being lazy instead of running with me.* Such animal tricks were for circuses.

Aidan yawned a few times, looked at his watch exactly five times, and eventually signaled to Paloma to call it quits. Her exit from the park was slower and more reluctant than when she came in. His steps, however, were determined, as if he had somewhere to go or someone to see.

After he left, I questioned my stupidity in being here. Unfortunately, the dark stranger or the alleged Marcel wasn't.

Deep within me, I needed to know if this was the same man as the BBC claimed.

If so, then what? Aidan might be in danger or unaware of this man's activities—and even if he was, he was harboring a terrorist. That was breaking the law, and came with many years behind maximum-security prison bars. But if that was the case, how would I go about telling Aidan? I thought about that all the way home.

The following night, I found myself there again, my question to myself still unanswered. Aidan talked at length with another dog owner who had a short, slow-moving bulldog named Rex. Paloma and Rex didn't see eye-to-eye. Each owner took turns releasing their dogs separately to do their business, while the other was kept on a leash. It started to rain. The light drizzle that had been forecast all day finally came, ending Aidan and Paloma's visit to the park.

By the third night, I'd begun to strongly doubt what I'd been doing. I couldn't keep this up. I'd become a stalker. I rationalized it with concern for Aidan's safety. Even as I approached the park, my doubts had grown deeper. More than once, I wanted to do a U-turn and return to the comforts of home—but my concern for the wellbeing of this man overrode that.

I guess that's what being in love does to you. You put someone else before yourself. No matter how much I tried to deny it, I was definitely still in love.

After all the rain we'd had yesterday and earlier today, a fog was slowly descending on the city tonight. It was warmer for this time of year. I guess that's why the fog made an appearance. It was great camouflage for my vehicle because the blown street light I normally parked near had been replaced. That area was now bright. It seemed like the other lights were brighter too.

I slouched in my seat and waited for his arrival around seven forty-five. Fifteen minutes later, Aidan hadn't showed. All the regular dog owners had come and gone. I wondered if he had come earlier because of the weather—but that would throw Paloma off her shit cycle. As the long hand on my watch approached the twelve, making it eight o'clock, he was already doing that. Maybe he'd taken her somewhere with him in that piece of shit car he had.

I had grown impatient and about to crank up my vehicle when I heard barking. It was Paloma. I could tell that bitch's sharp, howling bark anywhere. She was loose, as usual, which made me cringe on my leather seat. My displeasure soon dissipated, because Aidan approached with the dark brother. I sat up and squinted to see him more clearly through the lowering fog.

Yes, it was him. The same man. His head was bare, his short dreadlocks spiky, like a porcupine. His stride slow and confident. They walked side by side, laughing as if sharing a joke. They both held Styrofoam coffee cups in their hands, and took sips between bouts of boyish giggles. They seemed happy.

They sat on top of the damp wooden frame of a park bench. Fortunately for me, that particular bench was very close to a streetlamp that hit the bench like a spotlight. I took my camera and starting snapping away. The street light was my saving grace, as I couldn't use my flash—which I had previously worried about. I must have gotten a good ten shots in. I took out Marcel's picture from the envelope. Taking off my glasses, with my naked eye, I looked back and forth from the picture to his face. Yes. It was him. It was Marcel Bahati. The murderer. With this validation, a chill came over me.

As the evening fog descended to cloak them in intimacy, I turned the radio off and watched them embrace and kiss. I suddenly started the car, put on my glasses, and pulled out of there, speeding away, not caring if they saw me. I didn't want to witness them showing that kind of affection. I hoped he didn't recognize my car. But why would he even think it was me? We were broken up, and I was no longer a part of his life.

That night, sleeping was more difficult than usual. I kept seeing them together, kissing. Marcel with his hands and mouth on Aidan—the same hands that took innocent lives. It made me sick to my stomach, and I was determined to tell Aidan.

But after much thought, my more rational side began to explore the what-if's. Aidan might not want my help. He might resent me for delivering the truth. What if Aidan was a part of his organization? I began to scare myself with all those suppositions.

Eventually, I came up with a plan. I would return to the park and approach him, but only when he was alone. I would show him the picture of Marcel from the website, and bring him a copy of the story from the BBC website.

During the course of the day, I did a little research on the group Marcel was affiliated with. They killed because of their religious beliefs: suicide killings, beheadings, rape. This scared me, and I questioned if I should even get involved with such a man. But Aidan's safety was my primary concern. I tended to be loyal, and many had said it would be my downfall—because I couldn't step away from a cause.

I met David for lunch at a little restaurant downtown. He tried to make up an excuse to not come, expecting me to whine some more about Aidan. I told him that I needed to talk to him about a life-and-death situation. He sounded anxious, and wanted to know what it was. I insisted I would tell him all if he met me.

"You know, I had to pull some strings at work to come this early for lunch," were his first words of greeting.

"I know, and I appreciate you coming. You know I don't have that kind of flexibility at my job."

He hugged me, and so did the sandalwood musk he was wearing, which I hated. He settled in the chair opposite me. The look on his face was grave.

"Don't look so sad. I'm okay. This is not about me, but it involves me."

His shoulders relaxed, the graveness replaced as he rolled his eyes. "Oh, here we go. This does have something to do with Aidan."

"Yes, but it's not what you think."

"Isaiah, about that man, I've heard it all before from you. Frankly, I'm sick of hearing more."

"Hear me out, David. I didn't have you come here to waste your time. Not this time."

"What is it now, then?" he said with a tired look on his face.

"I've seen Marcel."

"Who?"

"Remember I told you about the guy Aidan was in love with in Paris?"

"The black French guy?"

"Yes. He's here in New York. I've seen him. Twice."

Then I proceeded to tell him about my trips to the small green neighborhood park in Williamsburg at night. He listened with a look of concern, which changed to exasperation as I repeated my nights of stalking. Then I showed him the picture of Marcel and the literature on the terrorist group. When I was done, the grave look on his face returned.

"Isaiah what have you got yourself into now?"

"What do you think I should do?"

"You know what the hell I think you should do. Stay the fuck out of it! But you're not going to do that, are you?"

"Aidan's life may be in danger."

"No, it isn't. But yours will if you get involved. You say that Marcel was the love of his life, and Aidan acted like he still was when you spied on them, right?"

"Yes."

"If he loves him like you claim, he's not going to hurt that man. I have a feeling that Aidan knows more than he's let you know. Why do you think he didn't want to talk about him when you asked? He was hiding this from you. He's hiding a fugitive. He's already created a prison sentence for himself. Leave this man alone, Isaiah."

Passionate and commanding, his words were resounding and final. I rarely saw David act like this. His concern was overwhelming, and I knew it was for my own good.

"What do you think I should do, then, just walk away?"

"Hell fucking yeah. Or report him, Marcel I mean—anonymously."

"I couldn't do that. It would land Aidan in jail."

"He's already done that on his own. Isaiah, this involves Homeland Security, and probably the FBI. This is no joke. This shit is serious. You're talking the federal government here."

"There has to be a way to not get Aidan involved."

"You're not listening to me, are you?"

"I am, but—"

"Bullshit! Call the fucking police, and do it now, before he disappears and blows innocent people up. How would you feel with that on your conscience?"

He had a point. Maybe I was being naïve. This had gotten more serious than I thought.

I don't have to get involved. I could walk away. There was a tug-of-war between Aidan and Marcel going on inside me.

David was right. But I couldn't bring myself to hurt Aidan. *What if David's hunch is wrong and Aidan is unaware of Marcel's connections?* I brought this to David's attention.

"Then let the authorities determine that," he said calmly. "You're in over your head. This is people's lives at stake here. They'll get to the root of it. There is a lot you don't know, or ever will. Let the professionals handle it."

The waiter brought our meal, and we both got quiet until he was gone. I had suddenly lost my appetite, and picked at my food. David looked at his watch and began to shovel his food in his mouth, barely chewing it. Between mouthfuls, he continued to encourage me to call the police.

"Let me think about it, David. Give me a little time. I'll do the right thing. Promise me you won't tell anyone about this."

"What the fuck! Are we in high school now?"

"David. Please. Just a little time."

"How much?"

"A week."

"A week? That motherfucker may be gone by then. What is there to think on this for a week?"

"Okay, two days then. Please, don't tell anyone."

"Fine. But you got two days. I got to go."

He got up, gathering his bag and coat from the back of his chair, dropping some money for the check. He turned to me before he left, and said softly, "You know I love you, boyfriend. You're my best friend, and I hate seeing you hurt like this. Do the right thing. Take care of you."

He turned and rushed out of the restaurant, and the

sandalwood odor followed him, leaving me more confused about my feelings than before.

I had no time to sort them out, because I now had a deadline. If I didn't do anything, David would call the police. I needed to know what Aidan knew about Marcel. But how was I going to do that?

CHAPTER FIFTEEN

That question remained in my mind all night, into the next day. I was anxious to let Aidan know, but then again, I was unaware of what he knew. I was concerned with how he would perceive me. I didn't want to appear desperate. David had forced me into this fucking deadline. I wasn't sure what he would do if I didn't meet it, and I didn't want to find out.

At work, I dreaded the approaching night. However, in one sense, I was excited to actually have a face-to-face conversation with Aidan—to look in his eyes, hear that voice and get a response. As I daydreamed about alternative outcomes, having a conversation with him was more important than the content. I had to figure out what I would say, and how I would raise the question of Marcel. I came up with a couple of scenarios in my head that seemed off. I tried writing them down, but it looked worse on paper.

I saw someone I believe to be a friend of yours on the TV the other night. Marcel Bahati. Do you know him? He's wanted for questioning by the police.

I discarded that note—how would I have known how Marcel looked? I only saw him in the park after we'd broken up. I attempted another one.

Have you ever tried to find the French guy Marcel on AOL after all these years?

I scrapped that one too. What reason would I have to bring up Marcel after he'd told me he didn't want to talk about him?

David's reasoning was beginning to make sense. I had no rational reason to bring up Marcel without looking like I was snooping—which I would be, at this point, because we were no longer dating. That thought didn't sit well with me.

As the end of my day at work approached, we suddenly got busy. I ended up having to stay longer to finish a couple of things—which turned out to be more than that. This project was more difficult than I'd calculated. All my stress was due to a particular client who was so fussy, it took several tries to please her. She found fault with everything from our color choices for her website to the font and the site's navigation.

My boss pressured me to meet the deadline, even though it was the client's fault we weren't on schedule. I thought my boss's unfair critique of the productivity of two people on my team should have been left for me to handle—which I eventually did. He knew that, but he liked to bust my balls just to show that he was in charge.

I rushed it as much as I could without alerting the coworkers that had to stay with me. At nearly an hour in overtime, I knew I wouldn't be able to go home and change before catching Aidan at the usual time. I would have to go directly from here. I hoped the traffic would die down by then.

Finally released, I rushed to my car, not caring what my coworkers thought anymore. One of them hollered something at me about being late for a hot date. It came from Dallas Burton, an overweight, middle-aged brother, who liked getting a rise from ribbing me. The teasing bordered on harassment. I'd considered going to HR, because it was beginning to get to me.

I jumped in my cold car, turned on the engine and waited, enduring the chilly air until the car started to heat up. I threw my jacket on the back seat and removed my tie and glasses, slipping them into the glove compartment.

On the way to Williamsburg, I must have been stopped by every red light. I wondered if this was an omen to discontinue my journey. I found myself shouting at slow drivers and giving the finger to taxi cabs cutting too close to me, as they always did.

I made it to the park in time, but couldn't find a parking spot. I drove around the block several times, but there were no spaces to be found. I double-parked in a dim area at the far end of the park, looking out for Aidan and hoping someone would move their car soon.

Then I spotted a police car patrolling on the other side of the park. This was the first time I'd seen them here. I revved up the engine and moved away from the park, onto an adjoining street, then turned onto another street. A vehicle was coming—the cop car, moving towards me fast. I moved as far as I could to the side of the street and slowed down, as if looking for parking.

Suddenly, he turned on his blue flashing light. *Oh shit!* I thought. *He's going to want to know what I'm doing in a primarily Hassidic neighborhood.* I was about to pull to a full stop, when the cop car increased its speed, sped past me, and whizzed down the street like a blue ball of light. I took a breath and let out a shallow sigh. Maybe that was another sign for me to take my butt home, but I couldn't do that to Aidan.

I made my way back to the green and saw a blue truck pulling out. I pulled up a car's length behind him, allowing him to pull out in front of me. I pulled into the space, turned off the engine and lights, except for the radio. I looked into the park and was surprised to see Aidan was already there.

He was sitting on a bench, looking in my direction, while Paloma pranced around. I couldn't make out his expression because it was in shadow. He continued to stare in my direction. His head did not turn either left or right, not even to keep an eye on Paloma. Did he recognize my car? Or was it simply that I was the only person out here that just parked a vehicle? He must be waiting to see who would emerge from the vehicle.

I suddenly got nervous. I had been busted—I think. Control of this situation had just been taken out of my hands. I sat there, unsure of what to do. I looked down to reduce the volume on the radio, and when I looked up, Aidan had gotten off the bench and was heading in my direction.

I panicked. Now I really felt like a stalker. I tried to calm myself as he got closer. I could see him squinting to make out who was in the car. When he was a few feet away, recognition and the look of surprise overtook his face. His forehead crinkled like a wave, and his lower jaw dropped. He was clearly shocked to see me.

I rolled down the window. "Hello, Aidan."

"Isaiah…" he paused, his face still filled with disbelief. "What are you doing here?"

"I came to see you. How are you?"

"I'm fine," he said dismissively, trying to comprehend my being there. "What about?"

"I wanted to talk."

"What about?"

I didn't want to have this conversation with him standing over me at my car window in a position of power, so I opened the door. He stepped back, and I got out of the car.

Now that I was at his level, I instantly felt better. Paloma barked from across the park, recognizing me, and bounded her way towards us as if to attack me.

"Paloma, stop!" he commanded forcefully. She reared up just before reaching us, her teeth gritted. She growled at me with a menacing stare.

"Paloma, shut up!" he commanded again. She whined before obeying. That bitch still couldn't stand me. Aidan turned to me and waited for an answer.

"I was on my way home, and on a whim, decided to see if you were out here walking Paloma."

"I thought you worked in Brooklyn?"

"I do but I was in the city."

"With your car in rush hour?" he quizzed me.

"I was off today. I had a job interview late this afternoon, and it took longer than I expected."

"Oh," he said, apparently unconvinced—but it was enough to stop the interrogation.

"So, how have you been, Aidan?"

"I've been fine, Isaiah."

"How's work? Gotten any new contracts."

"Work is fine, Isaiah."

"You seem a little mad at me."

"Yes, I am, Isaiah."

"I'm sorry. Why?"

"What do you fucking think, Isaiah?"

"There's no need to swear at me. I just wanted to see you to say hello."

"Hello," he said sarcastically, his eyes blazing and visibly angry.

"I guess this wasn't a good idea."

"What do you think? Why are you spying on me, Isaiah?"

"I'm not spying on you."

"Yes, you fucking are. I saw your car speeding away the other night. I convinced myself that it wasn't you, because what would you be doing over here in my neighborhood in the middle of the night?"

"I came to see you, but you had company."

He stared at me. On the attack, he'd put me in defensive mode.

I tried not to respond the same way he was acting. I struggled to calm him and explain myself. "It was obvious that the man you were with was more than a friend. I couldn't handle it. So, I took off."

He continued to look at me as if waiting for me to say more. I had said enough, and wanted him to respond. He turned to pat Paloma. The moments that followed seemed endless.

"Yes, that was more than a friend. Isaiah, you have to move on."

"I've tried, Aidan, but you're hard to forget."

"Try harder."

"I can't!" I surprised myself with my sharp outburst. He was making me get emotional, and I'd taught myself not to go there with him.

"It's over, Isaiah. I'm with someone else now."

"I know. I've been replaced."

"I wouldn't say that. You make it sound like I went out to find any man I could."

"It certainly seems that way."

"So, I'm accountable to you for who I sleep with now?"

"No. But I just thought it would take you time before you moved on, like I'm trying to do."

"Isaiah. I don't know how else to say it, but I have moved on."

The words came out of his mouth, stunning me into silence. I felt dumb, except for the rush I felt in my gut and the tears I tried to suppress. I was suddenly cold, the tips of my fingers like ice.

My body was heavy. I wanted to sit, so I did the next best thing and leaned against my car to prop myself up from falling.

"Are you okay?" he asked, somewhat surprised at my imbalance.

"Yeah, I'm okay."

"Are you sure?"

"I'm sure."

"Can I ask you a question?"

"Yeah. Go ahead," he said with reluctance.

"Who's your new boyfriend?"

"Isaiah. Don't go there. Besides, I don't think that concerns you."

"I want to know. It may help me move on."

"How?"

"It's just the way my mind works and deals with things. Facts help a lot."

"Yeah. I certainly remember that about you." He sighed and looked at me with pity.

"So, who is he?" I could almost see his mind debating over what to tell me. I recognized when he made the decision.

"We have history. I knew him long ago."

"How long?"

"Enough! I'm going to say goodnight and head home. You should do the same. It's suddenly gotten cold out here."

He turned and unhooked Paloma's leash strapped to his belt. He attached it to her collar as she slobbered and glared at me. They both turned to leave without saying goodbye or even looking at me.

"Is his name Marcel?"

He turned around quickly and looked at me. He didn't need to respond. My answer was in his eyes. They were filled with guilt, and his eyelids flickered nervously. He glared at me for a moment and turned, yanking Paloma's leash, then swiftly walked away from me.

His face and silence said it all. It was Marcel.

CHAPTER SIXTEEN

ow much he knew about Marcel's involvement in terrorism, I still didn't know, and I had no idea how to find out. He was clearly pissed at me. Another conversation with him wouldn't happen. He'd told me to move on. He wanted nothing to do with me.

I hadn't expected our meeting to go this badly. My fantasies had happier endings. I did need to move on, but how do you do that when you still deeply love somebody?

I barely remember how I made it home without having an accident; my mind wasn't on the road. After finally finding a parking spot two blocks away, my tired body tried to walk up the creaking stairs, holding the banister for support. The creaking of the stairs sounded exceptionally loud, tonight interrupting the quietness of the musty hallway.

Sure enough, Ms. Lucy's sliding door began to squeak open. *What is that woman doing up at this hour of the night?* I wasn't in the mood for her nosiness, and wanted to run up the stairs and shut my door before she got in the hallway. But that would be disrespectful. In some ways, she'd become an honorary aunt or grandmother, and I couldn't hurt her feelings.

"Who goes there?" she asked.

"It's me, Ms. Lucy," I said, turning around and sitting on a stair.

"That you, Isaiah?"

"Yes, ma'am."

"My vision is so poor these days. My doctor says I need bifocals, but those ugly things are so unsightly."

I knew what was coming next. She would go through a litany

of all her illnesses, and I'd appear interested and sympathetic. *Why do old people feel they need to bore people with all their ailments? You're old. Get over it. This is what happens at this stage in life. You should have lived a healthier lifestyle to lessen some of those illnesses.*

Ms. Lucy then stepped beyond her sliding door into the hallway, tying a bow at the waist of her antique silk nightgown. Holding onto the banister, she unsteadily made her way up a few stairs and plopped down next to me, smelling faintly of liquor.

A little out of breath, she exclaimed, "Chile, once upon a time, I could run up these stairs or do a fan kick to my ears." She chuckled to herself. Turning to look at me when I didn't respond as usual, she surveyed my face. "What's wrong, baby?"

"Oh. Just stuff, Ms. Lucy. I don't really want to talk about it."

"Hmmm. I see. Man trouble?"

No, she didn't go there. I was not about to talk about my love life with this old lady. That would be sacrilegious, like talking to my grandmother.

She knew I was gay. We'd touched on it before. She was a dancer. and lots of her male dancer friends were sissies. One of them who visited her on occasion tried to hit on me once. The man was old enough to be my grandfather. When I respectfully declined, he took it hard.

"Something like that."

"Baby, looks like he broke your heart. Did he?"

I wasn't sure how to respond to that. I'd already opened the door to my love life when I said I wouldn't. *What the hell.* Maybe she could give me some advice. She claimed she'd had many lovers between husbands.

"I don't know, Ms. Lucy. Maybe he did. I've never felt this kind of pain before."

"I know, baby. It hurts badly, doesn't it. All I can tell you is to embrace it. If you fight it, it'll hurt even more. Treat it like grief. Let it take you through the stages. I promise it will make you stronger at the other end. Life is to experience the good and the bad. You've obviously experienced the good with this man, to feel the way you do now. Try and think of those good times. It's a temporary fix, but it will work for those moments when the bad hurts the most."

"How long will it take to get over this?"

"That depends on you. Just don't be the victim too long, chile, or you never will."

"Thank you, Ms. Lucy."

"You're welcome, baby. Now, this old lady must rest these old bones. Goodnight, chile."

"Good night, Ms. Lucy."

I watched her totter down the stairs and into her apartment, pulling those heavy sliding doors together. I sat on the stairs a little longer, thinking about what she'd said.

That old biddy really gave me some good advice. Let's see if I can implement it.

I stayed in bed for the next day. David tried to contact me, reminding me about the deadline—but I didn't give a fuck. I didn't care what he thought or wanted to do with the information he had. Most of all, I didn't care about saving Aidan anymore.

It took a whole day of lying in a dark room for me to see all the signs I'd ignored.

He didn't want me. He hadn't for a while.

I was the rebound guy who reminded him of Terrence and Marcel. He never saw me. He saw aspects of them in me. *I am such a fool.* David tried to warn me, but I justified it by believing he was jealous because he had nobody. I'd overlooked David's honesty because I didn't like what he had to say.

I'd scheduled a medical appointment on the second day off work because I needed a note for work. As usual, I arrived late. Today, my doctor was running behind. Sitting in the waiting room, I filled out the obligatory questionnaire that was now on a clipboard. It consisted of the usual questions; if my insurance had changed, medical conditions, as well as a list of illnesses, including some dumb mental health ones that queried if I was depressed in the last week, and was I suicidal?

When I was done, I handed the clipboard to Jason, who registered me. I liked Jason. I'd seen him handle some very angry patients over the years with a smile and efficiency at clearing up their needs.

Finally, I was called. My nurse Pamela, a plump sister from Brooklyn who I also liked because she was funny, took me into a room to do my vitals.

"Isaiah, what is up with your blood pressure? It's high. What have you been up to?" she asked, concerned.

"How high is it?"

"One fifty-six over ninety."

"Wow! That is high. I've been stressed a lot lately."

"Well, you better do something to bring it down. Otherwise, he may have to increase your medication. Step on the scale, please."

I removed my coat and anything heavy I had in my pockets. I kept my boots on, because she allowed for that extra pound or so.

"Hmmm. You've lost weight, too. Almost ten pounds. Isaiah, please do something about that stress. Your numbers have been consistently good for a long time." Then she leaned over and whispered in my ear, "Don't fuck it up."

"I will, Pam," I said, smiling.

"You better. I like seeing you healthy. You're one of my favorite patients."

"Thank you, girl."

"Anything else going on with you that I need to know about?"

"I need a doctor's note for work."

"Why what happened?"

"I've been off for the last two days, and I intend to take one more. Let's just say it's for mental health reasons."

"Okay, I'll let the doctor know."

She left the room. It would be a while before my doctor showed up; he had to review my vitals and the information she was about to pass on.

About five minutes later, there was a knock on the door, and Dr. Jackson entered. He was a tall, slim older man who was in great shape. His pants were always tight-fitting, showing off his bubble butt. I suspected he was gay, because what straight man would wear tight pants in front of a bunch of predominantly gay patients? It seemed that the grey in his beard had increased since I saw him last. His greeting wasn't as cheerful as normal. He carried the concerned look that Pamela had.

"Afternoon, Isaiah."

"Hi, Dr. Jackson."

"Your numbers from your vitals concern me. What's going on?"

"Oh Doc, life. Just some stuff I've had some problems handling, but I'll be okay."

"Let me be the judge of that," he said sternly. "Your numbers show otherwise, and you don't want this to continue long-term. I see that you ticked on the questionnaire that this is mental health-related."

"It is. I want to take three mental health days, that's all. My job allows that."

"But Isaiah, in order for me to give you that note, I need to know why. If this is out of my hands, I may have to refer you to your therapist."

"Okay, Doc. My boyfriend and I broke up. He broke up with me, and he has someone else already, and I'm having a hard time with it."

"I see," he said, lowering his glasses on his long nose as he peered at me from above them. "I understand. Does your therapist know?"

"Yes."

"Are you working with him regularly to get over this hump?"

"No."

"Then I think you should, especially if I'm documenting a solution to your problem for this doctor's note. Will you make a series of appointments with him?"

"Yes, sir."

"How is your appetite?"

"I eat, but I'm not hungry most of the time."

"I need you to try to eat something. Even if it's something like soup, a salad, or even a pizza."

"I will."

"Based on your last results, your T-cells were 857, and your viral load is undetectable. Given the circumstances, that may change if we have blood drawn today. What I'm going to suggest is that we don't do that, because we know the numbers are going to be lower for the T-cells and higher for the viral load. Once you get a better handle on your situation, I want you to come back to do those labs. But if things don't improve with you in say about a month or so, come back anyway so I can gauge where your numbers are."

"Sounds like a plan, Doc. I'm good with it."

Then he listened to my heart with his stethoscope as I took deep breaths, looked at my eyes with his tiny flashlight, and had me push out my tongue and say "ahhh!"

Before he handed me the signed note, he put his hand on my shoulder and said, "You will get over this Isaiah. Trust." I thanked him and followed him out into the hallway. He shook my hand firmly, saying, "Take care. You're going to be all right. Just know this."

CHAPTER SEVENTEEN

went back to Jason at the registration desk to pay for my visit. After swiping my card and getting a receipt for it, I put both in my wallet.

"Isaiah!" someone called out from behind me in the waiting room, amongst the bowed heads filling out questionnaires. I turned around to see who it was. My name made everyone raise their heads, some only looking at me for a moment, then dismissing me as not their type.

Then he stood up and stepped away from behind a guy with dreads in a rainbow-colored Rasta hat. It was Cliff, a tall, light-skinned guy that I briefly tried to date a few years ago. I really didn't want to go over there and pretend, because I didn't like how he made me feel when it ended.

He looked good, though. His big pecs spilled out of his bomber jacket, and his cargo pants, though baggy, couldn't hide the definition in those thighs and calves.

He smiled broadly and waved me to come over, as if I was a long-lost friend instead of a reject he'd discarded. Reluctantly, I made my way to the last row of chairs, where he'd been sitting alone in the corner. He reached out to hug me. My response to his warm embrace was very restrained. Did this dude have amnesia? Did he forget how he'd treated me? Now I could only assume he was HIV-positive too; otherwise, why would he be here? He was holding a questionnaire clipboard in his other hand, which confirmed that suspicion.

"I thought that was you. I wasn't sure till I heard you speak," he said excitedly.

"Hello, Cliff."

"Man, you don't know how much I've thought about you, and here you are."

"Here I am. Looks like you conjured me up."

"Well, I need to do that more often to get what I want."

There was an awkward moment when he said this. He was excited to see me yet, he looked me up and down with a tight, suspicious grin. He'd obviously noticed my weight loss. I hope he didn't think I was sick with some opportunistic infection.

"So, what have you been up to?" I asked.

"I've been busy with school and work. It's hard, but I keep thinking of that end goal." Cliff was a very motivated, ambitious guy. I think he wanted to be a radiologist or paramedic. I didn't rightly recall. "But then this diagnosis happened, and now I don't know what to do."

"How long have you known?"

"Four and a half months."

"Do you have any support?"

"My roommate and one other friend. I'm too scared to tell my family."

"No. That wouldn't be a good idea. It's best you get used to it first before you start telling people, unless they're supporting you in some way."

"That sounds like solid advice. How long have you had it?"

"Oh! Years. I'm practically a veteran." I laughed to make light of it. He tried to smile along with me, but I could see that he wasn't at the point where he could see the humor in it yet.

"How did you deal with it?" he asked.

"I cried a lot at first, which felt like months. My eyes were always red from crying. I was so scared. I had horrific nightmares of how it would all end. I saw myself in a lot of pain and unable to take care of myself. I even dreamed the home health attendant ignoring me while she watched the soaps.

"Then I met someone here in this waiting room, and they persuaded me to join a support group. It was there I learnt to not consider myself a victim. I gained the knowledge that this was becoming manageable. Back then, it wasn't yet considered a long-term illness. There were a couple of people in the group who took me under their wing. They were my life-savers, because on more than one occasion, I'd considered suicide."

"Would you help me get to that place? I mean, in not feeling like a victim?"

To be honest, I didn't want to play teacher at this point in my life. I had my own shit going on. I didn't need someone else's. Then I thought, *You selfish bastard. It's now your turn to give back. What's wrong with you?* A sudden, overwhelming pang of guilt grabbed me by the chest, forcing me to relent.

"Sure. I'd be glad to help." The words forced themselves out of my mouth.

"Great! When can we hang?"

"Take my number."

"I still have it. See?" He scrolled to the contacts on his phone and held the phone to my face. "Is it still the same?"

"It is."

"Can I call you later?"

"Sure. Why not."

"It was great seeing you, man. You just made my day. No. It's more than that. You are the answer to my prayers. This time, He heard me." And he looked up briefly, clarifying that he meant God. Then suddenly, he reached over and hugged me again. Tightly. *Does this guy not believe in gentle hugs?* I caught myself being judgmental again and surrendered to his embrace.

Cliff whispered in my ear, "I'm sorry about how I deserted you. I guess karma is real."

Forcing himself to look me in the eyes, he partially released me from the hug as he finished whispering those last words, his face somber, his lips almost tremulous.

"Maybe," I responded. "But who really knows its true purpose? Maybe it's not as retributive as we think. I would hate to think that the universe or God is bitter, even though our religions teach otherwise. Some things have no explanation that we know of."

"I hope someday you can forgive me."

I patted his arm as I fully released myself from his embrace. "Talk soon," I said, and turned to head out of the waiting room.

Stepping into the parking lot, my encounter with Cliff remained uppermost in my mind—I felt uncomfortable with the after-effects of that hug. I needed human contact from someone who really meant it. Not from someone who was feeling remorseful and guilty.

Returning to work was tough. I pretended I was still getting over a cold, and faked weariness. My manager recognized that I was sluggish, and asked if I needed more time off. I refused, telling him that work would be the best thing for me right now.

It wasn't. I was second-guessing myself on decisions that would normally be effortless. I found myself rereading proposals I would normally understand the first time.

When I got home that night, I went straight to bed, but didn't sleep long, because I couldn't. There had been several messages from David again today, which I deleted. Cliff had called, but I was in no mood to inspire anyone right now. *I'll call him tomorrow.* After taking a shower, I began watching a sci-fi movie.

There was a loud knock on the door. I ignored it. But it repeated itself, becoming louder. I got out of bed, put on loose house slippers, and dragged my steps to the front door. Peeping through the keyhole, I saw the back of David's head. He was on his cellphone.

My phone suddenly rang in the next room. He was calling me. I almost went back to bed, but opened the door before he did something stupid, like call the police—if he hadn't already.

"Why haven't you been returning my calls?"

I looked at him wearily, turned without answering, and headed back to bed. He shut the door and followed me. He stood over the bed as I pulled my oversized comforter over my head.

"What's going on with you, boyfriend?" His tone gentler, trying another approach.

I still didn't answer. I just didn't want to.

"So, I'm getting the silent treatment. I have all night. I guess I'll just sit here until you do decide to speak."

He sat down on the edge of the bed pulling *Men's Health* magazine from the nightstand. I could hear him turning the pages impatiently and the faint smell of sandalwood being fanned by the turning pages. It wasn't as suffocating as the restaurant.

This uncomfortable silence continued. I knew I had to break it if I was to get rid of him, but I wasn't in the mood to be scolded for not keeping my word on the deadline.

"Did you call the police?" I asked, eventually pulling the covers from over my head and turning on my side, facing away from him.

"No," he replied. "I was more concerned if you were okay."

"Do you plan to call the police?"

"That depends on you, doesn't it?"

"You were right, if that makes you feel better."

"What do you want me to do?"

"Do what you want. I don't care anymore."

"Wow! That's a switch. What happened?"

"He's seeing someone else."

David didn't say anything. What could he say? He was the type to say *I told you so,* but didn't, for some reason. Instead, he reached over and gently rubbed the back of my shoulders, whispering in my ear. "Have you eaten?"

"No. I'm not hungry."

"Then do you want something to drink?"

"How could I drink alcohol at a time like this?"

"I meant hot tea or coffee."

"I'll have a hot cocoa instead."

"Coming up."

I could hear him puttering around in the kitchen, humming to himself. I was glad he was being patient with me, not asking me to fully explain what happened right now. I wasn't up for that. My cellphone rang. I reached over and picked it up from the nightstand. It was a number with no name, but I recognized those last four digits—8512. I had called it enough times, I'd memorized it—but I'd removed his number from my phone months ago. I hesitated before accepting the call.

In a confused state, I spoke, "Hello, Aidan."

"Hi, Isaiah."

"This is a surprise."

"I wanted to apologize for being rude the other night. I want to explain myself."

"You don't have to do that. It wasn't a good idea for me to have been there."

"It was a shock. But I'd like to make up for it. Can you come over so I can explain about the last thing you asked about?"

"Sure. When is good?"

"How about now."

"Now! Ah-hum. Sure, I'm not doing anything."

"See you in an hour or so then."

"Yeah. I'll be there."

He hung up the phone. I had sat up in bed during our conversation. The lethargy I'd been feeling disappeared. A spark of excitement replaced it. He called. He still had my number. He apologized. Then I looked up and saw David standing at the door with two mugs in his hands.

"How much of that did you hear?"

"Some of it. Was it him?"

"Yes."

I had gotten up out of the bed and was rummaging in my closet for something to wear.

"Where are you going?"

"He asked me to come over."

"Why?"

"He wants to apologize."

"Why couldn't he do it on the phone?"

"He wanted to explain about Marcel."

"Why couldn't he do that on the phone?"

"I don't know, David. I'm just glad that he's willing to talk to me."

"Isaiah, I don't like this. Something ain't right. You're getting all excited to go see a man that don't want you. He has Marcel. Isn't he the love of his life?"

"I don't care. I can warn him that Marcel is involved with terrorism."

"What makes you think he doesn't already know that? Didn't

that queen James say he had a shady past, and Aidan tried to shut him up? Aidan has to know."

"No, he doesn't. You're assuming things."

I already had gotten into my jeans and shoes and was now pulling a hoody over my head. David followed me out into the living room as I picked up my coat and keys.

"Isaiah, don't do this. It may not be safe."

"I'll be fine, David."

"Then where is his apartment? I'll go with you and wait in the car, just in case."

"That won't be necessary. I'll be fine. Lock up on your way out."

CHAPTER EIGHTEEN

rushed out the door leaving David gaping at me and shaking his head. As I headed to Williamsburg, I thought on what David had said. *What if Aidan does know; then what?* I'd noticed he didn't mention Marcel's name on the phone. Instead, he said, "the last thing you asked about." Why was that? I must admit David's question had created a little doubt in me, but it was too late now. I'd agreed to meet him, and I wanted an explanation for all of this. Who was I kidding? I also yearned to see him face-to-face again.

I rang the buzzer to Aidan's loft apartment. The buzzer was new. He had to come down and get me the last time I'd been here. I was buzzed in without a voice confirmation on the intercom. The hallway no longer smelled of urine or darkened by lack of lightbulbs, but was now clean and well-lit, with walls covered in bright graffiti. I climbed the stairs of the third-floor walk-up with trepidation, confirmed in my belief that there was truth to the saying about the fear of the unknown.

My steps were careful, if a little unsteady—at least in my head. I looked at the graphic graffiti on the hallway walls to distract me. Aidan had told me that it had been done by graffiti artists he knew. At first, the landlord would have the Super paint over it, but he came to realize that it was a selling point to most of his tenants, who were artists or creative types themselves. It was like going up a tunnel of slowly-moving pictures portraying urban blight and pride.

When I reached his floor, I hesitated before knocking. This was my last chance to turn the other way and run down this tunnel of stick figures and urban slang scrawled all around me. I crossed my fingers and knocked on his door. I heard footsteps approaching on the other side and multiple locks being unsecured.

The door to this fortress opened to an unusually passive Aidan, his body hid behind the door, as if for protection. He appeared as nervous as I was. I thought I was doing a better job of hiding my anxiety than him. It alarmed me to see him this way. I'd only known him to exhibit confidence at all times. Seeing this bashful side to him was disappointing. "Come in," he gestured with his head, standing aside.

I walked into his living room/bedroom and kitchen. It was one big room separated by furniture and drywall panels that ended a few feet short of the high ceiling. The place had not changed much, except that there seemed to be more of everything. The bookshelves were overflowing, a couple more pieces of awkwardly-placed street furniture added to the clutter. Multiple pots and pans continued to weigh down old hooks above the countertop. His bed was unmade. A book and an open bag of potato chips lay on it, waiting for him. In the kitchen, freshly sliced vegetables lay on a butcher's block. The strong aroma of the red onion was the most pungent.

Aidan resumed chopping the ends off broccoli, while I waited awkwardly for an invitation to enter the kitchen and join him, or to sit on the only stool tucked under the countertop. That invitation not forthcoming, I invited myself in and stood watching him work.

"Can I get you something to drink?"

"What do you have?"

"Orange juice, cranberry juice—I think, and water."

"Water would be fine."

He stopped chopping the vegetables, turned around to the refrigerator behind him, pulled out a small bottle of water from the door, and threw it at me to catch. I swiftly pulled my hands out of my pockets in time and caught the water, wondering why he didn't just hand it to me.

"Have you had dinner yet?" he asked.

"No not yet. I wasn't hungry tonight."

"Why's that? You gotta eat dinner, especially in your condition. You look thinner. Is everything okay?"

I was offended by this comment about my health. I had lost weight, but it wasn't because of HIV; it was due to the stress pining over him.

"I'm fine."

"You sure? You can have some salad if you like. I'll throw some tuna in for protein. My salads are really good. You've never had my cooking before, have you?"

Of course not, I thought. I hadn't been invited to taste his culinary skills because he hadn't stayed in my life long enough for me to experience that. This mild chatter was beginning to sound unnecessary to me. I wanted him to get to the point of why he'd invited me in the first place. But I knew I had to be patient. He had reached out, and I was at his place.

I watched him rapidly create a salad with everything thrown in: leafy green spinach, sliced carrots, mushrooms, black olives, red pepper, sliced red onions, olive oil and homemade dressing made from scratch, a secret recipe. He added crushed tuna soaked in oil and herbs. Skillfully, he tossed the salad and placed it neatly in a white bowl, sprinkling chopped cheese and dill over it.

Piercing it with a fork he handed it to me with a smile and indicated I should pull out the stool under the countertop. He stood, leaning back against the wall countertop facing me. We pronged and rummaged through our salads with our forks, chewing vigorously.

"This is really good."

"I told you," he said, smiling.

For the most part, our conversation was sporadic, and more directed at his cooking skills as we both worked on finishing his delicious salad. Then, halfway through, he realized he'd forgotten to add bread. He briskly heated up sliced French baguettes and slopped heavy wads of butter on them. It was delicious. I didn't know where my appetite suddenly came from, but this was the best meal I'd enjoyed in weeks.

My phone suddenly rang. It was David. I rejected it, and it went to voicemail. But it rang again. I repeated the previous step.

One thing had been bothering me: the absence of Paloma. I smelled her presence without her being here. I had expected her to pin me against the wall and slobber all over me when I'd arrived. However, I didn't miss the bitch. I was just curious about her whereabouts.

"Where's Paloma?"

"She's with a friend. What do you care? You've never liked her."

"That's not true. It was more the other way around."

"She tends to get along with most people, unless she senses that you fear her—then she takes advantage. I must admit she's a bully."

"I don't fear her. I'm just not a dog person."

We retreated to the living room/bedroom. He jumped on the bed with his shoes on and motioned me to sit at the foot end. There was no other place to sit. The only chair that I saw had painting utensils and canvas materials on it. I sat down on the bed and positioned myself as best I could, facing him with one leg on the floor, and the other bent and propped up on the bed for support.

Aidan was looking at me as if evaluating me. It made me uncomfortable. He lit a half-smoked cigarette in an ashtray on a makeshift nightstand that used to be a wooden crate. I watched him inhale deeply, then blow smoke rings into the air.

Then, with a fixed look that appeared stern or even cynical, he asked. "What do you want to know?"

This question came out of nowhere, blindsiding me. For a moment, I couldn't think of the right first question to ask. I had many but hadn't prioritized them yet. But I quickly pulled my thoughts together and asked, "Is Marcel your lover?"

"Was. Now I don't know what he is."

"What do you mean?"

"Your question; I answered it. I don't know if he is my lover."

"How could you not know?"

"It's complicated."

"I'm willing to listen and understand."

He looked at me in an irritated manner. I got it, I was being tolerated. This man didn't really want to see me. I still don't know what he wants.

"Why do you need to know? You're acting like a reporter or something."

"Facts work for me. That's how I process things."

He looked at me strangely. I assumed he was deciding what to tell me because a response was not immediate.

"I think I'm still in love with him. Didn't know that was possible after such a long time. He moves me like no man has. I get what he's about, and allow him to be himself. He does the same for me."

"What is he about?"

"Marcel lives for the moment. He rarely plans into his future. He is one of those 'now beings' that has no plan to his life, but things always seem to work out."

"How is it possible to not plan in this day and age? Doesn't he have ambition? Is there nothing he wants to do or achieve?"

"No. He believes that Allah will provide direction. Like he always has."

"What direction is Allah guiding him to here in the States?"

"What are you asking me? Your questions are very personal. What are you up to, Isaiah?"

"I'm up to nothing. Just curious, that's all. I think you know how I was feeling about you. I want to put closure to it."

"Was feeling? As in past-tense. Are you sure you're being honest with me?"

"Yes. I'm sure."

"Then why were you spying on me in the park? Why are you here now?"

"You invited me."

"Yes I did, didn't I? But I didn't expect you to come. I was surprised at how quickly you agreed to this meeting. It isn't my intention to lead you on."

"I'm here to work on closure for myself. I'm not a fool, Aidan. It's obvious your life doesn't include me, and hasn't for some time. Did it ever? Were you ever really serious about me?"

His features seemed to sag from the weight of the question. I couldn't tell what his eyes were saying—he hid his feelings very well. I prepared myself for whatever truth he was about to reveal about our relationship. In the last few minutes, I had lied about my true intent towards him. I wondered if he'd do the same.

"I cared—once. But I found you judgmental. You have an opinion on everything. I found your opinions to be absolutes. There were no grey areas with you. It was stifling. I'm not that guy. Isn't who I am, what attracted you in the first place? I'm a free spirit. Marcel gets and accepts that, because he's the same way. You, my friend, are of the Establishment. You're really very conservative, even though you try to be liberal."

His words hurt. My whole being was in full denial of his perception of me. *Everyone has opinions. Aren't I entitled to have them, too?*

How was I judgmental of him? I loved and adored him. I liked that he was different from me. I liked his intensity. I wanted to respond verbally with everything I was feeling and saying in my head, to defend myself from this unfair attack.

But it was as if something in me said to leave it alone. *It's too late. Let it go. Move on.*

"Wow! Well, I guess you told me," I said, making light of it.

"I'm not trying to hurt you with the truth. You know me to be honest. That's who I am."

"But I don't think you've been honest with me."

"What the fuck! I've just told you the truth and why it wouldn't work with us. What more do you want?"

"You haven't told me the truth about Marcel."

Suddenly, Aidan jumped up out of the bed and stood over me. I didn't like the menacing stare that penetrated me. His hands balled by his sides, as if he was ready to use them. "What do you mean?"

I couldn't back down now. I had come here to confront him, and had avoided it. I couldn't let fear make me back down. I stood up. We faced each other, our noses inches apart. I could practically feel his breath descend on me from his slightly greater height. His chest heaved and released more controlled breaths of anger.

"I think you know what I mean."

"No. I don't. Why don't you tell me?"

"Let's not play this stupid game, Aidan. I can tell by your actions that you know exactly what I mean."

"No, I don't."

"Your man Marcel is a terrorist, Aidan."

"I don't know what the fuck you're talking about."

"I think that you do." Out of my pocket, I pulled a folded FBI mugshot of Marcel and shoved it at him.

He looked at the picture. His expression was emotionless. "I think you should leave."

"Aidan, you're concealing a known terrorist. That's a federal offense."

"Get out of my apartment."

CHAPTER NINETEEN

e both maintained the same defiant stance, our faces still inches apart, waiting to see who would back down first. Who would be the weaker man, first to retreat? Just then, I heard a key opening the front door at the far end of the loft. Paloma bounded into the room, and seeing me, growled.

"Paloma, heel!" Marcel said, walking into the room.

"He knows," Aidan warned Marcel.

Marcel's smile of greeting swiftly disappeared. He rushed across the room, leaping at me, as Aidan stepped out of the way. He knocked me down, and we landed hard on the bed. I could feel the full weight of his body on me, and his knee in my groin. I cried out in pain, trapped below him, unable to clutch and console my balls. It hurt so much.

He was stronger than me. I could feel his body weight forcing me into the bed. He grabbed my cheeks with his large right hand, digging his thumb into one and stabilizing the other forefinger in the other. He squeezed them hard, bringing his face close to mine. Two dark pupils surrounded by the wide-open whites of his eyes, peered at me with hatred.

"You are the infidel I've heard so much about," he said in a rough French accent.

I didn't respond. I couldn't. His fingers still squeezed my cheeks inward like a vice. And even if I could, what could I say?

"Marcel, let him go. This isn't the way."

"What other way is there? He knows my identity."

"Let's see if we can work something out. Let me talk to him."

"You already did that. Now it's my turn."

Marcel released his fingers and punched me hard across the face. I cried out. Tears welled in my eyes as I brought my hands to my face to console the blow. He hit me again. The second blow hurt harder than the first. His knuckles separated my hands, striking my cheeks to the bone. Blood spurted from my nose.

"Stop, Marcel! Let me talk to him!"

"Nah! Let me kill this pussy."

"Please, I won't tell anybody," I pleaded.

"Shut up, pussy-boy!" Marcel yelled. "Or you'll be sorry."

My cries turned to whimpers. I couldn't force myself to be quiet. My face and groin hurt. Blood was on my hands and clothes. The sting of both attacks festered.

"Marcel, arrête ! Ce n'est pas comme ça que nous avons décider de régler cette affaire," said Aidan in French.

"Et ben, ta manière ne marchait pas, donc là je m'occupe de ça à ma façon."

"Non ! Sans violence. Tu m'avais donné ta parole."

"J'ai changé d'idée."

They were speaking in French. A few words sounded almost English, but of course, I didn't know what they were saying. They looked and sounded as if they were arguing. I thought Aidan was trying to defend me.

My jaw was becoming numb. It hurt to a lesser degree, but the pain remained. Marcel was very passionate and did a lot of pointing at me that I knew was not complementary.

"Marcel, he was my friend."

"The cause does not have friends."

"He won't do anything to harm me."

"No. I won't. I swear," I interjected.

"Shut up!" Marcel shouted at me.

"Then we need to figure out another plan," Aidan stated.

"There is nothing to figure out. Il doit mourir."

"No, Marcel. There has to be a better way."

"What is wrong with you, Aidan? Whose side are you on?"

"Yours, mon amour."

"Then tie him up."

Aidan reluctantly went into the kitchen and returned with

duct tape. He unraveled the roll and cut a few strips with scissors. With his head, he motioned for me to get off the bed. I stared at him in disbelief, feeling betrayed that he wasn't fighting harder for my release. I slowly pushed myself to the end of the bed and stood up. The blood I had wiped on his sheets smeared, drying on my face and hands.

Aidan quickly turned me around and pulled both my hands behind my back. He doubled the tape and wrapped it around both my crossed wrists. I could already feel the tape sticking to my flesh as he tightened it. My blood rushed to that area. Then Aidan got the stool from the kitchen and helped me sit on it. Marcel came behind me and checked his handiwork. He tugged on the tape roughly. It dug into my skin, making me flinch. I dared not groan like I wanted to.

"Now what?" Aidan said, looking at him.

"Let me make a phone call," Marcel said, drawing out his cellphone and heading to the bathroom. He left the door partially opened. I could hear him speaking very low in French. What was it that he needed to hide from Aidan? I was aware that Aidan was straining to hear what he was talking about—though he pretended he wasn't—while he wiped the remaining blood off my face with a damp rag.

"Aidan," I whispered. "Someone knows I'm here."

"Who?"

"A friend."

"What friend?"

"You don't know him. You two never met."

"Does he know?"

"Yes."

Why did I say that? I wasn't going to give him David's name, but I wanted him to know that someone knew I was here.

"You've put me in a difficult position. But it's your fault for meddling. It's out of my hands now."

My phone rang in my pocket. Aidan froze. Marcel rushed from the bathroom, still on his cellphone.

"Take that phone from his pocket," he ordered. Aidan did as he was told. "Who is it?" Marcel demanded.

"It's David. His best friend," Aidan said, reading the screen of my phone.

"Let it go to voicemail." Eventually, the ringing stopped, but it rang almost immediately afterwards again. David obviously hadn't left a message.

"Silence it!" screamed the highly irritated Marcel. "Does he know, too?" Marcel demanded of me.

"No, he doesn't," I quickly responded.

"You better not be lying to me."

"I'm not, I swear," I said after a brief pause. I looked Aidan's way to see if he would deny my lie. But he didn't. I sighed inside with temporary relief.

"No one knows."

"Marcel. I think you should get out of here, just to be safe," Aidan said.

"I'm working on that now. But your little friend here could snitch on you."

"He won't. He won't hurt me. If you hurt him, it will let the police know you're in the States. They don't know where in the world you are now. Why jeopardize that? The more anonymous you are. the better for you."

Marcel thought this over. He'd hung up his cellphone. He shook his head as if he agreed with Aidan's reasoning, but didn't say anything.

The tape was beginning to hurt around my wrists. I had fallen on my hands on the bed when he rushed me, and he seemed to have hit my hand when I tried to protect my face from the second punch. It was tender now. I attempted to adjust myself on the stool to ease the discomfort I was feeling all over.

I wished I had given David Aidan's address, as he'd requested. All he knew about my stalking was that it took place in a small neighborhood park in Williamsburg. I wished he'd called the police. They would have been here instead of me to arrest or kill this crazy fool.

Marcel's cellphone rang again. He retreated to the bathroom to take it. Minutes later, he returned, incensed. Whoever was on his phone got him angry.

"We must interrogate him."

"Marcel, I think you should get out of here."

"Not until I know what he knows." He pointed a finger in my face haphazardly and clipped my nose, causing it to bleed again. Unable to stop the blood myself, I looked to Aidan to wipe it like he did before. But as the blood crawled down into my goatee, he didn't move or even make an attempt.

"Who knows who I am and where are they?" Marcel screamed in my ear.

"No one," I whispered, now genuinely scared.

He grabbed my blood-stained cheeks and sunk his fingers into them as the middle of his hand smothered my face. My nose was raw. It hurt. I wanted to cry out. It took all I had not to. Then he released my face and went into the kitchen.

Marcel returned, kicking one of Aidan's wood crates out of his way. Aidan watched with grave concern. Marcel had a pitcher in his hand. Water spilled from it as he approached me. I had little time to wonder what he was doing before he grabbed my head, tilting it back roughly and pinching my nose.

I couldn't breathe except through my mouth. The pain in my nose was excruciating. It was like having a tooth pulled with no anesthetic.

He squeezed my cheeks again, forcing my mouth to form a pout. Cold water rushed into my mouth. I was thankful for the water in my parched mouth, but he kept pouring faster than I could swallow. I struggled to close my mouth, but he kept forcing it open. I couldn't breathe. It was icy cold. I could feel my body seize up from the pressure. My body was in shock, and so was my mind.

This whole experience was surreal, as if I was in a live movie and had no control of the outcome. I wanted to bite his hand, but I couldn't. I couldn't be humiliated by this beast. I started to cough as water continued to rush down my throat. I spat it back out, tightened my throat, and squeezed the muscles very hard to fight the onslaught of the water.

Lashing out with my feet, I began to fall off the stool, but he held me firmly from falling. I coughed violently, spitting out the icy cold water.

Then he stopped. The water had run out. I let out a hacking cough. I felt like I was choking as excess water sputtered out of my traumatized lungs, forcing me to cough even louder.

"Go refill this jug," Marcel ordered Aidan, "and add ice to it."

I swear, through teary eyes, I saw Aidan hesitate at the latest command. But then he snapped out of it and rushed into the kitchen. I heard the water rushing in the sink. I heard the freezer being opened.

Marcel was still holding me, and put me back on the interrogation stool. "You will tell me all you know now, or the next test will be fire."

My body cringed at the thought of this. Was he for real? This wasn't the Soviet Union. I wanted to cry out, but couldn't. The thought of fire so unsettled me that in a reflex, I rose suddenly from the stool, pushing through his arms—but lost my footing and went hurtling to the floor. I pushed my right shoulder forward, so as to not hit my head first.

My shoulder crushed into the ground. I swore I must have dislocated it. Instant pain hurtled through my body, as if I'd been electrocuted. It was unbearable. I howled, screamed hoarsely. I didn't care, not anymore. Screaming was the only release from the spasm of pain that shocked and shook my body.

"Shut up, punk!" Marcel shouted back at me.

But I continued to howl and kicked furiously on the floor, while he dodged the kicks that could take him down. My face hurt; my shoulder, devastated. Pain invaded my body from many directions.

"Help me!" I yelled out, hoping that a neighbor or someone would hear me.

"Shut up, you fool!"

A hand clamped down over my mouth to stifle my shouts. I bit into it. It was swiftly removed by the shrieking owner. The shrieking belonged to Aidan. I continued to kick and scream "Help! Help me! Somebody."

I was like a rabid dog in the deepest throes of its disease.

Someone kicked me in the stomach. It winded me. I started to cough. My body was all contorted on the ground, my hands still tied behind my back. I couldn't remain still. I moved to avoid the pain, but encountered more of it. I was in too much agony, and I was in no position to listen to orders to stop moving; it hurt so much.

I sensed that they had given up trying to silence me—for the moment, anyway. Through the tears that smeared my eyes looking up I saw the blur of their bodies above me, trying to stay clear of my kicks, which now had become a reflexive action from the pain that continued to torture my body. As my vision grew a little clearer, I perceived that my captors were in a panic. My unconscious outburst was a total surprise to them. They seemed lost and mentally disoriented. My wrestling on the ground, even though it made the pain worse, couldn't stop me.

Something within me snapped and told me to do this to stay alive. But even if I didn't want to, my body was doing otherwise. I had lost control of it. It controlled me. It continued to defend me.

CHAPTER TWENTY

uddenly, my body was being lifted from the ground by the shoulders. The hands holding my shoulders hurt like hell. I tried to kick them, but I was exhausted. I had become hoarse from the screaming. All the power I had in protecting myself by lashing out was diminishing as my body was lifted onto the bed.

"Here, take this. It's Motrin; it will ease the pain," Aidan said as he put two tablets to my lips. I opened my mouth and welcomed them in, followed by room-temperature water that was slowly sifted in, not forced like before. After I was done, he gently pushed me back on the bed, on my side. Some pillows were there to cushion my descent.

"Relax. Let the medication sink in."

Aidan's voice was very soothing and kind, even though the pain was vivid. It felt more comfortable to keep my eyes closed, which left me reliant on my other four senses. For the first time, I noticed that my hands were free and beside me. They were stiff, as if they had gone to sleep. The blood slowly began to circulate in them. It was weird, uncomfortable and painful.

I wanted to go to sleep. My body was compelling it, but my mind reminded me of my situation. I had to stay awake or I might never wake up again. Even though he'd made no threats to kill me, I didn't trust him. He was a terrorist and capable of anything. I fought the compulsion to give up and fade away into the unconscious.

The pain lessened a little. I figured the Motrin was kicking in. That was probably what was making me sleepy along with my exhaustive exhibition on the floor. I had to stay awake. My eyes shot open and I tried to sit up. Aidan pushed me back down.

"Lie still." He said.

Some of the pain had returned in my attempt to right myself. I succumbed to his request. I could feel Aidan's presence beside me watching me. I lay still. The pipes to the radiator began to rumble.

Then I heard a muffled voice far away. As my senses got keener, I recognized the tone. It was rough and argumentative, speaking in French. Marcel was still around, probably in the bathroom, talking to the person from earlier on his cellphone. I knew this was my opportunity to appeal to Aidan—find out what was going on or what their intentions were.

I whispered to him, "Aidan. Please help me."

There was a pause before he answered, "I'm working on it. Don't worry."

His words, though comforting, were not enough. He probably was sincere—but Marcel was in charge.

"Who is it that he keeps talking to on the phone?"

"A contact."

What did that mean, *a contact?* I needed to know. I had to know. "Another terrorist?" I asked.

"Hush. He'll hear you."

Those words confirmed to me that Aidan was being genuine about my wellbeing. In a way, he was protecting me from his friend and ex-lover. The love of his life.

Maybe Aidan had an idealistic view of Marcel's affiliation with this group, but was now seeing the dangerous side of him for the first time.

Marcel wanted to belong in a country where he wasn't wanted because of the color of his skin and parents who rejected him for who he chose to love—that, I understood. But what I didn't get was him being part of a radical group and being gay. How did he pull that off? He could definitely pass for straight, but in time, that could catch up with him.

"Aidan?"

"Yeah?"

"This is not who you are."

I looked at him when I said this, gazing at him with puffy eyes.

He paused. He looked like he was about to respond in some truthful way, but didn't. He ignored my statement and looked away. Perhaps it was to hide his shame. I also wondered how he planned to get me out of this mess, because all he'd done was sit there.

The bathroom door creaked as Marcel lumbered into the room. He scanned the room with an angry glare that rested on me. The way he looked at me was very

demeaning.

"What do you have to eat?" Marcel asked Aidan.

"A tuna salad."

"I need meat, not leaves."

"All I have is leftovers."

"What?"

"Mutton stew from the other night."

"Yeah that would do. It was good."

I wondered if that was something he was allowed to eat as a Muslim, and if he couldn't, him breaking the rules wouldn't surprise me. He was already doing that with his sexuality.

Aidan had gone into the kitchen, and was heating up the stew. He didn't microwave it but poured it in a pan and put it on the stove. He turned around leaning against the counter and looked at me. I couldn't see what his eyes were saying but I did not get his attention for long.

"Did you get through?"

"What?" Marcel said, obviously distracted with his own troubled thoughts.

"Your call."

Marcel looked at Aidan but didn't respond. The intimidating glare that Aidan received was enough for me to translate that Aidan needed to keep his trap shut in front of me.

From that unspoken communication, Aidan's body language changed. I could almost see his shoulders drop, his head fall. He quickly folded his arms, and then released them, turned his back and slowly stirred the stew.

"Marcel, I think you should go," Aidan said, his back still turned. "It's not safe here for you."

"Will you shut up?" Marcel said, almost under his breath.

I watched the muscles in Aidan's shoulders tense. He stopped stirring the soup for a moment, then resumed. I could tell when he was about to speak because his back would heave upwards.

"I need for you to leave, Marcel. I can't be a part of this."

"I know," Marcel responded softly.

"Then why stay?"

"Because it is not time for me to leave. Not yet."

What did that mean? Did this have anything to do with me, or some other terrorist activity? I know I had become a problem or liability for Marcel. I was doing my best to stifle the fear I felt within, but it was becoming increasingly harder to do.

It was like Marcel was waiting for something. Maybe advice or directions. He wasn't in charge. Someone else was calling the shots. If that was the case, how could Aidan effectively appeal to him on my behalf?

Aidan turned off the burner. The soup was ready. He poured it in a bowl. Steam rose from the hot stew. He put it on a tray and slowly carried it to Marcel, who was seated on the wood crate he'd kicked out of his way earlier.

I don't know if I imagined it or not, but there was a pause before the tray was handed over to Marcel. In my mind, I thought he would throw the hot soup in Marcel's face. But that was not to be the case.

There wasn't a *thank you* from Marcel. He took the tray and immediately slurped his first mouthful, dunking a piece of baguette in the stew and blowing on it before it disappeared in his mouth. He didn't look like he was enjoying the soup this time. I seemed to occupy his senses more. With each mouthful, the intimidating stare became more frightful.

When he was done, he put the tray down on the floor, then checked his cellphone, as if someone had called him. I didn't hear any kind of ring or buzz or vibration. I looked at him through swollen eyes. Suddenly, there was a call. He stood up and darted to the bathroom, speaking French.

It made no sense to me for him to take refuge there, because I couldn't understand what he was saying anyway. Then it dawned on me—Aidan could.

"I thought you were working on him," I muttered to Aidan.

He looked at me. From the expression on his face, he was figuring out something, and having a hard time doing it. There was no look of satisfaction showing if he'd had an idea.

Marcel emerged from the bathroom with a triumphant smirk on his face. "He'll be here shortly."

Aidan nodded acknowledgment. *Who? Who'd be here shortly?* I wanted to know. I wanted to say something, but it seemed like the Motrin was a little too strong, more like a sedative. *What did he give me? Did he lie to me?*

I willed myself to stay alert. I attempted to sit up on my good elbow on the bed but the pain from the other arm wouldn't let me. I remembered seeing some survival reality show, when someone was in a similar predicament—but they were battling the elements and not people. I began to deep-breathe as silently as I could so they wouldn't notice. The breaths tickled my nose. I was afraid it would lead to bleeding again, so I transferred the breathing through my mouth.

In and out. In and out. In and out. The whole idea was to send oxygen to my brain to keep me alert. I wasn't sure if it was working yet, but I wasn't falling asleep. Not yet, anyway.

I thought about who might be coming. It had to be the contact Marcel was talking to on the phone, or someone else that worked with their organization. Another terrorist showing up? This was not good. I wouldn't stand a chance.

My only hope was Aidan. But was he telling the truth? Was he really working on getting me free?

CHAPTER TWENTY-ONE

The room had fallen into anxious silence. Through my swollen nose, my forced breathing was amplified through my entire head. Then the doorbell rang, startling all of us. I instantly became afraid of the unknown. Whoever had rung that bell took their time to come up. Eventually, there was a harsh tapping on the loft door. Marcel leapt to his feet and hurried to the door. Aidan gave me a brief, tense look. We both looked towards the door as we heard the final latch open.

We heard Marcel's greeting of reverence in French. A gruff response to his greeting followed, which sounded dark and ominous judging by the low tone, like that of a chain smoker. We heard a series of taps slowly making their way to the living room before their source entered.

His scent flooded the room first. I wasn't sure what it was, but it wasn't pleasant. There was one final tap, and he was in view.

An old man leered and sniffed at us suspiciously. He reminded me of Shylock in Shakespeare's *Merchant of Venice,* a cataract in his right eye, peering at us from within its deep cavern below bushy grey eyebrows. His long, angular nose still sniffed at us like that of a rodent. A stark maroon beard covered most of his lower face, and disappeared into the clothing on his chest. His simple white robe matched the tightly-wound turban that sat on his head like a crown. An old leather coat hung limp off his shoulders. The old walking stick that was his guide dog looked as ancient as he did.

"So, this is the infidel," he growled, sounding like he'd just had a hookah hit.

"That is him, Brother Abdul Hamid," Marcel said, glaring at me.

"And who is this?" he asked, pointing his stick at Aidan.

"He is a friend."

"I see," Abdul Hamid said, turning to look at Marcel curiously. "He is white."

"I know, Brother Abdul Hamid. I've known him for many years, since Paris. He can be trusted."

"Can you be trusted, young man?" Abdul Hamid asked Aidan as he leaned forward, his blue cataract flashing in the lamp light.

"Yes sir, I can be trusted," Aidan mumbled, trying to sound confident—though I was sure he was as intimidated by this creature as I was.

"You speak French?"

"Yes, sir."

"Address me as Imam Abdul Hamid."

Aidan shakily called him by his name, including his title. He was obviously having a hard time hiding his anxiety, which was not lost on Marcel.

"He is not the issue," Marcel said, trying to bring the attention back to me.

"You are too trusting!" The imam snapped at Marcel, shooting him a fiery look as Marcel bowed in shame. "No one is to be trusted until they prove themselves."

"That is correct, Abdul Hamid. I understand."

Then Abdul Hamid turned his attention to me. He moved closer to inspect me. The odor I had smelled was stronger—the rancid smell of an old man who wore no deodorant.

"Do you speak French too?" the imam asked of me.

"No, Imam Abdul Hamid."

"How do you know this man?" the imam said, pointing a clawed finger at Aidan.

"We are friends."

"And Marcel?"

"I don't know him."

"Are you sure? Don't lie to me, boy."

"I just met him today."

"But I understand that you do."

"I don't know him, Imam Abdul Hamid."

"Your friend says that you do."

I started to sweat, thinking about Marcel's crumpled FBI mugshot in my pocket. I didn't know if I should throw Aidan under the bus or not.

But he'd already done it to me. How much he shared, I wasn't sure, because they'd spoke in French.

"I only know of him from what I saw in the news." I said.

"And what is that?"

"That he is a part of Al Qaeda."

"Go on."

"And he is wanted by the FBI overseas. I don't believe they know he's here in the States."

Imam Abdul Hamid listened to what I said calmly, except for his wheezing. He must have been asthmatic.

"How do you know that?"

"Because that's what the reporter from the BBC said."

I hoped and prayed that Aidan hadn't told Marcel about the picture I'd shown him.

"And you. How long have you known?" Imam Abdul Hamid pointed his stick at Aidan again.

"I also only know what I've seen on the news, Imam Abdul Hamid," Aidan responded, with more confidence this time. I breathed a sigh of relief.

"It wasn't a shock to you that your good friend was a known terrorist?"

"It was. But I understand his struggle. I know his history, and sympathize with some of his beliefs."

I was shocked to hear this. I wasn't sure if he was lying to save his ass or if he truly meant what he said. Then Marcel jumped into the conversation.

"Brother Imam Abdul Hamid, when Aidan told me what he saw on the TV and I explained to him the truth and not the lies Western media spins, he understood."

The imam still looked skeptical. He hobbled over to the crate and sat on it. He fell into deep thought as he mused over what he'd heard. I think we all waited anxiously to hear his conclusions.

Instead, he reached into his coat and dug into his pocket, looking for something. He pulled out a pill bottle and struggled to open it. Seeing this, Marcel went into the kitchen. The imam opened it and put the bottle and its top in his lap, while he suckled on what looked like a lump of dark chocolate, peering at Aidan and I from under those thick eyebrows.

Marcel returned with a glass of water, handing it to the imam as he slowly tilted his head backwards and threw two pills into a mouth full of rotten teeth, gulping down the water to wash them down.

Minutes later, the pills and the sugar appeared to have revived him. I began to wonder what was going on with his health. Was he diabetic? Or did he have something more serious going on?

"Is there a room where we can speak in private?" the imam said, addressing Marcel.

"Yes. Sure, Brother Abdul Hamid, come this way."

The imam stiffly rose from the crate and slowly followed Marcel to the bathroom. This time, he closed the door. Ideally, this would be my moment to escape, if Aidan would take this tape off me. But then he would suffer the consequences of helping me, which would mean certain death. I didn't put it past these two to take me out.

The thought of that sent a shiver through me. At this point, I had to think about myself. I wouldn't be here in Aidan's apartment if he hadn't lured me in.

"Aidan," I whispered, "we have to get out of here."

"We? And where am I to go? This is my place."

"To the police. We don't stand a chance with that imam here now."

"It will be okay. Marcel will speak to him."

"I don't trust the old man," I whispered sharply. "We know who Marcel is. We both admitted it to him. Do you think he's going to let us live, especially as the authorities don't know where Marcel is?"

"Marcel will protect me."

"And what if he doesn't? It's all about their agenda. They kill innocent people all the time."

"You don't know Marcel. I trust him. He'll find a way."

"Maybe for you, but what about me? He couldn't care less about me. They are probably in there plotting how to dispose of me. I'm scared Aidan. Please if you ever had any feelings for me, do something. Take this tape off me."

Aidan grew silent. He looked really confused. The assertiveness that was my experience of him had disappeared. He looked like a confused child.

"I can't do it. Trust me. I'll figure something out. But I can't let you go."

My whole body drooped in disappointment. The fear inside me amplified. This was really it. I was about to be executed, and didn't know how it would be done. My mind raced with random thoughts of doom. The hope I'd clung to under Marcel's interrogation began to fade.

A dark wave of foreboding energy gripped my body. The impending numbness was winning over the will to survive. The feeling of helplessness was pervasive. I was surrendering to it.

We heard murmurs coming from the bathroom. Angry outbursts were coming from the imam at times, but it was all in French.

"What is he saying?" I whispered to Aidan.

Aidan hesitated before he answered. He did not look at me, but strained to hear what was being said. "They are talking about other matters."

I found this hard to believe. What other matters could be more pressing than this one causing the imam to be angry? Aidan wasn't telling me the truth. What he was hearing was more dire than he was willing to admit. It only deepened the depression I'd sunk into.

"I don't believe you. Tell me the truth."

"Shush! I am telling you the truth," he said, still not looking at me.

I got quiet, allowing him to listen, seeing it was futile anyway. I began to face the reality that I wouldn't get out of here alive.

CHAPTER TWENTY-TWO

thought of all the experiences I'd miss. The little things; like the buttery taste of French toast mixing with syrup in my mouth, or that first early morning latte, the rough texture of hot sand on a beach exfoliating my feet, getting a fresh haircut, or the softness of my little niece Amanda when she ran into my arms, and clamped her chubby arms around my neck.

My musing was interrupted by the creaking of the bathroom door opening. The imam slowly emerged back in the room and sat on the crate, back straight, in a regal manner. His cataract eye switched from Aidan to me before he spoke.

"You have complicated things for Marcel and me. I don't believe you're telling me the truth," he said to me. "You must have told someone else about Marcel. Now I need you to tell me, who?"

"No one else knows," I said in sullen resignation. I didn't care anymore. I was doomed, and words wouldn't save me now.

"You're lying!" shouted the imam, spit flying in my face.

"He's telling you the truth, Imam Abdul Hamid," Aidan said, coming to my rescue.

"How do you know this?"

"Because I've known Isaiah all my life. We are like brothers. We grew up together. He doesn't lie. He is too religious for that." Out of the corner of my eye, I could see Marcel's mouth drop, but he did not interrupt.

"A filthy Christian."

"Yes. He is, and his beliefs are honest and good, just as I'm sure your beliefs are. I know he respects and honors the beliefs of others, even though different than his own."

The imam listened to these brave words spoken by Aidan in a forthright manner, and with much humility.

I was impressed. He was trying to help me by lying about our past. A tinge of hope reassured me.

"Then we must disagree. *Allahu Akbar !* Nothing else matters. *Tuez-le Marcel !*"

Suddenly. Aidan jumped in front of me. "No!" he shouted.

Marcel pointed his gun at me, but stopped as Aidan blocked his target.

"Move, Aidan," Marcel shouts.

"*Tuez-le, Marcel !*" The imam shouted again.

"No, Marcel. Don't shoot him," Aidan pleaded.

"Shoot them both!" the imam demanded, pounding his cane on the floor. "Do it, Marcel. What are you waiting for? Shoot the Christian devil!"

Marcel lifted the gun again, but then stopped halfway. His hands shaking, sweat plastered his forehead. The imam's patience was quickly waning and he dug in the pocket of his coat, pulling out a small semi-automatic pistol. Raising his arms, he shouted, *"Allahu Akbar !"*

The ear-shattering sound of the gun echoed throughout the loft, immediately followed by another shot. The smell of gunpowder punctured the air. A scream and a grunt accompanied the shots. Aidan and the imam's bodies fell to the hardwood floor, both crying out in pain.

Marcel ran to Aidan and sank to his knees. I couldn't see if he was still alive, because Marcel's back was blocking my view. All I could see was Aidan's limp legs, which weren't moving.

"Aidan! Aidan!" Marcel desperately called out to him.

Then one of Aidan's legs, twitched followed by the other. "Marcel…" I heard Aidan say. As he found his bearings, his voice sounded weak.

"You're alive!" Marcel exclaimed.

"Yeah. My arm hurts like hell."

"It looks like the bullet grazed your skin, missing the bone."

"Please, stop the bleeding. Tie something around my arm."

I quickly handed Marcel the long strands of duct tape that had held my hands captive. He grabbed them and wrapped them around Aidan's arm. Aidan suppressed crying out as he tightened it. Marcel grabbed a wash towel, which he firmly placed over the wound.

"What about the imam?" Aidan asked.

For the first time, Marcel looked at the restless body of the imam, groaning and muttering something in French. Marcel gently set Aidan's upper body down and kneeled beside the imam.

Blood was everywhere, creating a randomly splashed tie-dye design all over his robe. His body shook in spasms as he struggled to breathe. Trickles of blood flowed out of his mouth. The spasms suddenly stopped. The body stilled.

No one knew what to do. We all stared in shock. Then Marcel put his hand into the bushy beard, to the neck of the imam and tried to feel his pulse, but the imam suddenly cringed. His breathing was labored, tributaries of blood flowing from his chest wound. Marcel reached out again, and was stopped by a violent spasm.

"He's still alive. What have I done!" groaned a distraught Marcel?

"You saved me," Aidan said. "How can we help him?"

"I don't know. Give me a moment to think," Marcel said. He was losing it. The old man must have meant a lot to him.

"You should call an ambulance," Aidan suggested.

"Are you mad! And say what? How would I explain this?"

"We'll figure something out, but you have to do it now."

"If he was to survive, he would have someone else finish the job on both of us. No, we must let him die."

Aidan wearily let his words sink in, I could tell it wasn't something he wanted to do. "Then we must make him comfortable to meet his maker," he said pragmatically.

Marcel gently lifted the imam's head up and put his turban under it. A cascade of untamed red hair surrounded the imam's head like a bloody halo. "Imam, I'm so sorry, but I could not let you kill my friend."

The imam didn't respond. His breathing had become raspier. A gasping sound replaced the low groans he'd been making. "Do you hear me? I'm sorry," Marcel repeated.

The imam's eyes slowly opened. The blue cataract eye, now bloodshot, flashed as if searching to focus. Eventually, his eyes settled on Marcel. He mouthed to speak, but words were not forthcoming. He tried again, forcing the words to make a sound. It was calm, with the intent behind them very clear and filled with animosity.

"You traitor. Allah curse you all the days of your life." The words struggled out of his mouth, hissing from the lungs of the dying Imam. "You are weak, and not a true man."

"Imam, what do you mean?"

The imam's eyes closed, but continued to twitch. His lungs exploded in a fit of coughing. He started to shake uncontrollably. Marcel tried to steady his body, but the shaking was incessant. Suddenly, it ceased. The coughing stopped, and his body went limp, falling silent.

There was no need to check his pulse. The imam had made a painful transition to meet Allah. Then Marcel did the sweetest thing. He took the imam's clawed, bloodied hand, and held it in both of his.

Aidan and I watched as Marcel prayed over the imam, rocking gently as he murmured to himself.

"He's gone," Marcel said eventually, and carefully released the imam's hand from his, laying it gently by his side.

We both looked at Marcel as if to say, *what happens now?* Marcel was still looking lost, grief adding to the confusion on his face. He walked towards the window, rubbing his hands through his short, wayward dreads. We watched him stare out the window, muttering a low chant to himself. I wasn't sure if it was in French or Arabic. *Do Muslims even speak Arabic?* I didn't know, but it sounded like a foreign murmur.

"Marcel," Aidan addressed him. "I'm so sorry."

Marcel turned around slowly, drained and looked at Aidan in a tired manner. It was like what he'd done for love was sinking in, and the weariness seemed to ask if it was worth it.

"We have to dispose of the body," he said, ignoring Aidan.

"I don't think that's a good idea."

"Then what do you suggest, Aidan!" Marcel said, raising his voice.

"I don't know."

"Then shut up!"

"Don't talk to me like that."

"How do you want me to speak to you?"

"Not in anger. Not after what you just did."

"Don't remind me. It was a huge mistake."

"What are you saying? That you should have shot me?"

"It would have been a lot easier, wouldn't it?"

"You don't mean that."

"Look. Right now, I need you to work with me, not against me."

"I'm trying, but being angry at me won't solve anything."

"I think after what I just did, I have a fucking right to be angry. Don't you think?"

Aidan shrunk in defeat. Marcel was right; he wasn't helping. I didn't see a solution that would end favorably for him, either. Disposing of the body of a mentor whom he obviously respected would haunt him. But he chose Aidan—love was stronger.

CHAPTER TWENTY-THREE

The tension that had overwhelmed the room was interrupted by the sounds of sirens in the distance. The sirens were multiplying, getting closer and louder. Marcel ran to the window—the sirens sounded like they were mere blocks away.

"It's the police!" he shouted. "I gotta go."

"Yes, get out of here," Aidan told him.

"But the imam…"

"Don't worry, I'll figure out something."

"I have an idea," Marcel said. "Tell them the truth, but stretch it a little. Tell them he shot you because he suspected you knew about *the cause.*"

"But how do I explain him knowing where I live?"

"I told him where you lived and I was staying here. He came to warn me that the FBI knew I was in the country and was hot on my trail. Tell them the imam had me beat up your friend to find out what he knew. I shot the imam in self-defense of you."

"But why would you do that?

"Because we were old friends from Paris. I was visiting, and you knew nothing about my connection to *the cause.*"

Aidan began to protest that the cops wouldn't believe him, and there were too many holes in the story, with not enough time to think them through. Marcel went to him and hugged him gently, avoiding hurting his arm. Holding Aidan's head in his hands, he softly kissed him on the lips.

"Tell them, if you have to, of our love. They know that my faith strictly forbids homosexuality. I wouldn't share being a part of *the cause* with anyone because I'm sworn to secrecy. One secret is bad enough."

"But when the press puts that out, you will be a target by those in *the cause* as well."

"I know. I wanted to get out. The imam knew this, and rejected it. I witnessed cruel things that I was a part of, and could no longer tolerate. I am no longer part of *the cause*."

"Where will you go?"

"Don't worry about me, *mon amour*. I have endured much, and am a survivor. And you," he said, looking at me, "please tell the FBI what I've said. I know you love Aidan, and in feeling so, you'll protect him from any suspicion of being an accomplice. Promise me that."

"I promise," I said, having no choice.

"I'm sorry about how I treated you. It was out of jealousy, because I see you still love him. Forgive me."

I nodded, even though that was not what I was feeling.

The police sirens now sounded as if they were at the end of the block. "I love you, *mon amour*." Marcel said as he turned from the windowsill of the huge loft windows.

"I love you, too."

He unlocked the window and stepped onto the fire escape turning around to take a final look at Aidan, blowing him a kiss with one hand and nodding farewell to me.

Aidan looked crushed but there was no time to dwell on it. The police would be here any minute, and he had to be strong. I had just promised to lie to the police to protect a terrorist who'd beaten me up, and was in love with the man I'd loved.

"You don't have to keep that promise, Isaiah. It is a lot to ask of anyone, and I won't hold it against you."

"No. It's okay. I'll keep my word. I think it's a good plan."

"Are you sure?"

"Probably not, but I think it's the right thing to do."

"Even though we just said we loved each other in front of you?"

"It was hard, trust me, I won't lie—but we don't control love."

"True. You're a good man, Isaiah."

"Thank you, and I believe you to be, too. But enough of all this sentimentality—let's go over our story before the cops get here."

We quickly went over what Marcel had suggested—agreeing to say as little as possible, sticking to the facts we knew, and knowing nothing about *the cause.* I destroyed the mugshot in my pocket by ripping it into small pieces and flushing it down the toilet.

Suddenly, there was a loud banging on the door, and a commanding voice said, "FBI. Open up!"

I looked at Aidan. He gave me a look of encouragement, and I nervously went to unlock the door. As soon as the latch was free, the doors burst open, ramming me to the ground. The heavy body of a man jumped on top of me, forcing me to turn over on my belly. The equipment he carried around his bulletproof Kevlar vest and waist dug into my skin. He roughly grabbed my hands and handcuffed them behind my back. *Oh no, not again.* I was feeling déjà vu once more.

In the background, I could hear Aidan shouting in my defense. But they were not listening. My head was turned to the side on the floor under his raw hands. I saw the combat boots of officers in their jackets with big FBI logos on their backs as they invaded the loft, arms holding AR-15 rifles as they cased the place, shouting "Clear" after finding no one in the bathroom.

"Officer, I'm not who you're looking for, I'm innocent," I managed to say as my mouth squished against the hardwood floors.

"Shut the fuck up!" his gruff voice said in my ear.

They surrounded Aidan. They called him "Sir" as they asked him questions while two paramedics tended to his wound.

Other agents roughly rummaged through the loft, looking for evidence. They were wrecking the place; everything got capsized, opened, upturned and discarded recklessly to the floor. Someone told the officer on top of me to get off. The officer lifted me to my feet. My wrists hurt from the handcuffs digging into the previous wounds.

I was able to see Aidan's face amongst the officers that

surrounded him. He saw me looking, and was about to say something to me, but an officer asked him a question.

Suddenly, the ear-shattering sounds of gunshots were heard in the distance. All the FBI agents stopped as the rapid fire continued for a few more seconds before ending. Someone communicated something through the earpiece of one of the officers. The officer simply said, "We got him."

I caught Aidan's eye. At that point, the life drained out of his face, turning into a vacant stare. I detected a slight tremble to his lips, as if he wanted to cry out, but suppressed it. His head then drooped to his chest. He became non-responsive to the officer's questions, seeming to be in a world that no one was invited to. Eventually—after the insistence of the paramedics who needed to get him to the hospital—the officers gave up.

Wheeling him out on a gurney, I caught his eye one more time. The desolate look I saw in them scared me. I whispered *I promise* as they led him away, but I didn't think he comprehended it.

The officer who held me read me my Miranda rights, then roughly escorted me down the graffiti-painted stairway to the street.

I was immediately blinded by the flashing lights of the police cars, firetruck, and ambulance. The flashing camera lights of the press added to the irritation. How did they get here so fast? A crowd jeered and verbally hurled obscenities. Multiple police and FBI agents were on their cell phones or radios. A cop had a megaphone, and tried to control the crowd.

I was shoved through a makeshift corridor lined with the bodies of officers protecting me as we hurtled towards a vehicle. I looked around to see people peeping from their windows, straining to see what was going on. The crowd that had gathered stood behind yellow caution tape. Many of them were Hasidic Jews looking at me with judgmental eyes from beneath black yarmulke. I heard a woman scream, "that's him, he was always hanging around here!" The crowd jeered even louder.

I turned to see whose mouth those caustic words had come from. It was the woman from the square who wore the green scarf and grey tracksuit with the Labrador. She looked at me, defiantly shouting, "I knew you was up to no good." The officer escorting me pulled me away from her and pushed me towards the waiting vehicle.

Above all the noise, someone shouted my name. I saw David rushing towards me. A couple of FBI agents stepped in his way.

"I was the one who called you and told you where to find him," David protested.

"Let him through," said another agent.

David ran up to the still-open passenger door and leaned in to…but they wouldn't let him touch me.

"Oh my God!" David exclaimed. "Your face, what did he do to you?"

"The imam commanded Marcel to do it. How did you know where to find me?"

"You said a green square in Williamsburg. There were several, but when a neighbor in this building called about hearing gunshots, the detective and I headed over here," he said, indicating the detective that stood behind him, the one that had said let David through.

"The gunshots we just heard a short while ago, were they…"

I didn't have to finish the sentence, because David was nodding in the affirmative. Our conversation ended as the door was slammed in his face and the police car pulled away, leaving David looking helpless and troubled.

CHAPTER TWENTY-FOUR

was taken to an FBI precinct somewhere in Manhattan and grilled with endless questions for hours. They sometimes repeated the same questions, but in a different way, as if it was a personality test for a job. In a small, depressingly drab interrogation room, with old furniture and the smell of stale coffee, I was interrogated under a bright fluorescent light that made me sweat from its radiant heat just above my head.

When I got tired, they gave me coffee. When I was hungry, I got a sad turkey sandwich with only mayo and white bread. Eventually, I figured out they were trying to see if I was part of *the cause* or an accomplice. I didn't know what David was doing on the outside, but I wished he'd get me out of here—could he? I'd become irritated by one particular FBI agent with the thick eyebrows, piercing blue eyes, and a faint Southern accent.

I asked for a lawyer. I was told I could get one, but under the Terrorism Act, they could hold me longer than usual. What I didn't know until later was that they had to accuse me of a crime, and I was guessing they had nothing.

Eventually, I was escorted along a labyrinth of halls that led upstairs to a cell, where my handcuffs were taken off before they pushed me in. The walls were bare cinderblocks. There was nothing in there but a narrow twin bed, its thin mattress and a flat pillow covered by a worn sheet. An attached, open stainless-steel toilet and sink were riveted to the wall. A half roll of toilet paper stood on a simple shelf. The cement floors were bare, without any tile to cover their nakedness.

I was left alone with my thoughts and the distant sounds of

doors slamming, unclear conversations, footsteps, and keys jingling. I lay back on the bunk bed and closed my eyes, trying to relax, but I couldn't. All that had happened to me in the last twenty-four hours or so crowded my brain. I was in jail, the reality of that was sinking in and I got scared, really scared.

My imagination rushed me forward to years of being behind bars, molested, beaten up, starved of good food and verbally abused. I turned to bury my face into the slim pillow without a pillowcase, recoiling at its rancid smell. I eventually settled down and dealt with it, because who knows how long I was to be here?

"Isaiah! Isaiah, wake up!"

I jumped up, startled, blinking from the bright fluorescent light above. Someone was peering in at me from the glass window in the door. I blinked, trying to make out their features. I'd obviously been asleep. A key went in the keyhole, and the door opened. A tall, slim guy stood outside beside an officer.

"Thank you, Agent Brooks. May I come in and speak with you, Isaiah? I'm your lawyer."

"Sure," I said, still dazed and unsure of what was going on.

"I am your court-appointed lawyer. I'm with the ACLU, and will represent you."

"I can't afford you."

"Don't worry about that. I'm working pro bono. Do you know what that is?"

"Yes, I do," I said curtly, ticked off that he underestimated my intelligence.

"Okay, then, I didn't mean to offend you."

"I'm good."

"Now Isaiah, I know you have gone over your story a thousand times with the FBI, but I need to hear it from your lips. I need to know everything in detail to defend you."

"My story is the same as I told them."

"Okay. Let's start from the beginning. What were you doing at Aidan's loft, and how do you know him?"

I visibly rolled my eyes at having to go through this again, but this guy was the first one who'd been kind to me since this situation started. He sat beside me on the bed with a manila notepad on his lap and a pen ready to scribble notes. I painstakingly began to recount this ordeal. Occasionally, he'd interrupt for clarity.

This time, telling it I felt like I was reliving it all again, and the light brown eyes of this guy hung on my every word. He cringed when I told him about the beating I'd gotten from Marcel. However, I remembered Marcel's advice to tell as little as possible, even though this man was my lawyer. I trusted no one except David.

When we were done, the lawyer went over the preliminaries of what I'd have to go through. He told me he'd contact me as soon as he did some research.

"What is your name?" I asked as he banged on the door for Agent Brooks.

"My name is Terence Simmons. Everyone calls me Terry. I like that; it's less formal."

"Okay. Thank you, Terry."

"You're welcome, Isaiah. See you soon."

The door slammed, the key in the lock turned, and he and the agent left.

On the hard bunk that night, I had problems falling asleep, even though I was tired, but eventually I did. I dreamed of the cold-eyed FBI agent grilling me.

"How do you know Marcel Bahati?"

"What is your relationship with Aidan?"

"What were you doing at the loft?"

I woke up covered in sweat, with an uneasiness in my gut. I was in custody of the FBI. I was under suspicion of colluding with a known terrorist. This is not good. The gravity of my situation began to weigh on me. I couldn't spend the rest of my life in jail for not being that, even though lying to the FBI could put me there.

I smelled. I still had dried blood on my clothing, and I needed a shower badly. My aching body craved to be in my own bed, devoid of nightmares.

Early the next morning, I was awakened by banging doors and raucous laughter echoing down the hallways. I got the same nasty turkey sandwich, with the most bitter coffee I'd ever tasted. I spat it out immediately. I was even afraid to have a shit, because I thought I was being monitored.

A new agent came to get me. *Where is Agent Brooks?* I wondered. He didn't put handcuffs on me, but instead, ushered me out of the cell into the hallway and followed me, telling me when to turn right or left. Where were we going? Why didn't he handcuff me? I started to worry, because this was making no sense. He followed me through the labyrinth of corridors again, unlocking doors as we went. We finally got to a door that was different than the others. It had exit above it. He unlocked it, and told me to step through. I tentatively did so, as if stepping into a lion's den on the other side.

Three men who were conferring, with their backs to me, turned as they heard the big steel doors open. David stood a few yards away with the detective from before and Terry. David and Terry were smiling at me. My heart leapt. The joy rising inside me in that moment, I could never forget. I didn't know what they were about to tell me, but it had to be good.

"Isaiah, how are doing, buddy?" David said as he embraced me. I held onto him so tight, I didn't want to let go, but did abruptly. I wasn't about to embarrass us at the station in front of heterosexuals who hated faggots. "We need to get you home to shower. You smell funky," David joked. I cracked a smile. I know it was hard for him to see me this way. I'd seen it on his face both yesterday and now; I understood him making light of my situation.

"I can go home?" I asked David.

"You're a free man, thanks to the help of these two gentlemen."

"Hello, Isaiah, I'm Detective Cuomo. We were able to check into your background, including family, friends, employers, etcetera, and everything checked out. You have no connections to any terrorist group."

"Isaiah," Terry said, "we were able to prove that you are an upstanding, productive American citizen, even with that misdemeanor arrest from the park incident. That had nothing to do with what the FBI was seeking. It was to see if you have any affiliation with any terrorist group or was being recruited by them. Luckily, with the help of Detective Cuomo, we were able to prove it without you going to court."

"Go home, Isaiah. Get some rest. You're a free man. However, we will call on you to be a witness when the need arises," said Detective Cuomo as he firmly shook my hand and disappeared behind the door from which I'd come.

Terry moved closer to me, and in a low voice just short of a whisper said, "I must warn you that the news has gotten out to the press, and some of them are waiting outside to question you. Say nothing. David and I will escort you to his car. You will have to deal with them camped out in front of your place for a while, so David thinks you should stay at his apartment until things calm down."

I could smell Terry's cologne. It was Emporio Armani; I'd recognize that scent anywhere. *Terry has expensive taste.*

My gaydar had awakened, and I began to pay attention to this very attractive guy with the smooth skin, pretty brown eyes, and short afro. He was relaxed and less formal than when the detective was present. I began to suspect that he was family, and was I kidding myself that he might be attracted to me? But he'd embarrassed me by mentioning the park arrest. Was that really necessary to bring up now?

"How is Aidan doing?" I asked David. They both exchanged glances that looked suspicious.

"He's still in the hospital. They're keeping him a little longer for observation."

"Is his arm okay?"

"Yes, it is."

"David, there is something you're not telling me. What is it?"

"Isaiah, he hasn't spoken to anyone since he heard the gunshots."

"I must see him."

"No. That wouldn't be a good idea."

"Why?" I asked, pissed that I wasn't getting the full story.

David and Terry exchanged the same looks again; then Terry jumped in.

"Isaiah, the doctors suspect that the history of mental illness he had may have returned. He's being seen by a psychiatrist as well."

"Oh my God!" I gasped. "I must see him."

"Isaiah, like David said, it wouldn't be a good idea. Not now."

"His parents are with him," David said, "and I don't think they'll want you to see him."

"But why?"

"They seem to think that you had something to do with triggering his relapse into this deep depression."

"I had nothing to do with it. He's depressed because he lost Marcel, the love of his life."

I noticed David giving Terry a furtive look again before he said. "They don't fully see it that way. It may take some time before they're willing to accept the truth."

"Isaiah." Terry rested his hand on my shoulder and gave it a firm squeeze. "Right now, you must take care of Isaiah. You have some challenging weeks ahead, and it will be a while before things return to normal."

"But his parents kicked him out. They don't understand his lifestyle."

"He is still their only child, and it appears they are overlooking that. They are doing the right thing. Family comes first."

"Isaiah, I need to get you home. Come now." David put his right arm behind my back, steering me towards the exit. For the first time, I became aware of the stares of random officers behind the desks, judging me.

Flanked by David and Terry on either side of me, with my head bent forward, we pushed our way through aggressive journalists who blocked our path. The questions they fired at me were short and blunt.

"Isaiah, how did you come to know Marcel?"

"Who beat you?"

"Who killed the imam?"

"What was the imam doing at Aidan's loft?"

"What were you doing at Aidan's?"

"What is the nature of your relationship?"

"Isaiah, who was sleeping with who?"

"Isaiah, are you a homosexual?"

That last one got to me. I paused, wanting to turn around and scream "yes!", but David tightened his grip on my arm and pushed me to his car. We got in, locked the doors as David fumbled to put his key in the ignition hole. The vultures surrounded his car, snapping pictures and shooting rapid-fire questions. They had gotten personal, and were more interested in my sex life. Apparently, my arrest in the park had gotten out, because that was public knowledge—especially now that I was a newsworthy.

I buried my face in my hands to hide from the flashing glare of the cameras as anguish stiffened my body. I thought I was about to have an anxiety attack.

Terry held the back of my neck and rubbed it with his thumb to help me calm down. David maneuvered the car through the vultures and sped up the street. Terry gave David directions on which way to go in order to lose any of them who might be following.

CHAPTER TWENTY-FIVE

The next day, I woke up in David's bed. I looked at my watch on the bedside table. It was one o'clock in the morning. I must have slept for about twelve hours or so. I still felt tired. I lay there listening to the light drone of early morning traffic outside. Where was David? The bed felt so good, I didn't want to get up and find him, but eventually I did.

David was on the sofa. He'd fallen asleep in front of the TV, which was still on. His reading glasses resting on the tip of his nose, about to fall off any moment. I gently removed and folded them before putting them on the coffee table. I pulled the throw rug up closer to his chin. while he softly snored. I didn't know what I would have done without this man. He'd rescued me so many times in my life.

My best friend had become my dad. The most humiliating thing I'd had to do was to call him from prison to be bailed out when the park incident happened. I was still paying off my debt to him. *I'm so grateful to have this man in my life. Yes, I'm truly blessed.*

Later that morning, I spoke to my boss, who'd been informed of what was really going on, and not what was in the news. He was very supportive and understanding. He told me to take as much time off that I needed, which surprised me, because that man loved to make money off my labor.

"Terry called to check on you last night while you were asleep," David told me.

"Oh really! That was very nice of him."

"I think he's sweet on you, in a professional kind of way."

"That's all it can be—I'm his client."

"But when you're no longer that, who knows?" he said, giving me a wicked smile.

"Look at you. I'm just freshly out of jail, and you're trying to marry me off."

"You got a lot on your plate. A little distraction won't hurt."

"You're no good."

"I know, honey," he said, winking at me.

I wouldn't watch the news. I was breaking news. All three of us were. At least Marcel wouldn't have to deal with the backlash Aidan and I were getting. The conservative radio and TV stations focused on our sexuality, as if that was the cause of everything. The liberal ones didn't care so much, but it was news, and added a juicy element that wasn't the norm for a terrorist headline.

They dug into my background and tried to interview my family in England, but they refused. I hadn't spoken to them yet. I was dreading it. What a horrible way for me to come out to them. I wondered how Mama was feeling. I was angry at myself for disappointing her the most. I did what I'd done all my life. I avoided their calls with excuses done by others on my behalf until I was ready to face them with my truth, which was no longer my own.

It had been robbed from me, and sold around the world. Gay groups rallied around me and Aidan. GLAAD was organizing a fundraiser to help towards Aidan's hospital bills. I was asked to be the guest of honor, but I declined. Terry stepped in on my behalf.

I said to him one day, "It feels strange calling you Terry. It's so personal, and you're my lawyer."

"I wondered when you'd get around to asking me that. Would you prefer to call me Mr. Simmons all the time? That would make me feel so old. I'm not that guy. I'm most comfortable in jeans, sneakers and a T-shirt."

"This I'll have to see," I said, smiling.

"Maybe you will one day."

The tone of his voice was playful when he said this, but he looked me directly in my eyes without wavering as if communicating something deeper that I was supposed to understand. I looked away, because it made me uncomfortable. I knew what that look meant.

Finally, I had to force myself to call my family and explain myself. It was a lot to unload on them, and I was feeling guilty about it, because it wasn't fair. I had run myself a bath in order to calm down. It did help initially, but as I dialed my aunt's number, that tightness in my gut returned.

My cousin James answered the phone. I was relieved that it was him to break the ice, so to speak. When he heard my voice, he burst out laughing. "Hey cuz, I see you've become gangster, as they say in the States, messing with terrorists and all that. I didn't think you had it in you. Much respect."

"James, believe me, this was no picnic."

"I'm sure, mate, but you made it through. You're a hero."

"Hero! I don't think so. If anything, I'm a victim."

"That's not what the papers are saying over here."

"Ignore that shit. Some of that stuff is made up."

"Does that include the part about you being gay?"

"Well, that's what I called to talk about."

"I don't have a problem with it. You're my cousin, you're family, and we love you."

I was surprised and touched by James's candor, which was short-lived because I could hear Aunt Brenda saying in the background, "I don't."

"Shut up, Mom!" James scolded her.

"Boy don't tell me to shut up. This is my house, and you will have some respect."

"Can I talk to her?" I asked James.

"You sure you want to do that? Besides, she says she don't want to talk to you."

"Then let me speak to Mama."

"She's upstairs. Let me call her for you. Olivia! Tell Mama she has a phone call. Her grandson, you know the celebrity from America," he joked.

"Oooh! Isaiah. I want to talk to him." Olivia shouted back. "Mama! It's Isaiah. Hurry, he's calling from the States."

I could hear Olivia bounding down the creaking wooden stairs and being confronted by Aunt Brenda.

"Bloody hell, what's your rush. I don't know what's wrong with you kids he's brought shame on the family."

"Get over it, Mum and let us enjoy his five minutes of fame," Olivia responded.

"Fame! For what?"

"Oh hush, Mum. He's a celebrity. He helped get a terrorist."

"I don't care about that. I've been fending off questions from nosey family members for weeks, and not even a word from him."

"Oh Mum, they can piss off then. They ain't real family if all they want to do is judge," James said in my defense.

I was listening to all this, and no one had yet made it to the phone. Finally, Olivia picked up.

"Hi luv, how are ya?"

"Not good, judging by Aunt Brenda's response."

"Oh! She'll get over it. She's just being a sourpuss right now. But listen, are you going to do any interviews? Has Barbara Walters called?"

"No, Olivia. I'm trying to put this behind me, if only the press will let me."

"But why not milk it for all it's worth? You could get paid for interviews. Be on magazine covers. You'll meet all kind of celebrities, and of course, someone will offer you a book deal."

"Book deal?" I laughed. "I can't write."

"Don't worry about that, hon, that's what ghostwriters are for. Isaiah, take my advice. Trust me on this. You could be set for life. I can just see the blurb on the book jacket. *A homosexual interracial love triangle with another man who happens to be a terrorist.* It would sell millions."

"Olivia, you're nuts."

"Maybe, but think about it. Don't let this be a missed opportunity. Mama's here. Bye."

My high-spirited cousin got off the phone and handed it to my grandmother. I could hear the phone rustling before she got it comfortably to her ear.

"Isaiah, darling, how are you doing?" Her voice sounded weak as she forced some cheeriness to it. I liked when she called me darling; it always sounded like she was singing it.

"I'm doing okay, Mama, considering."

"I know, son, I've been praying for you."

"Thanks, Mama."

"It must have worked, because you're alive."

"I hadn't thought about that, but you might be right."

"Ain't no might about it, child. It's not your time yet."

"Yes, Mama. I wanted you to know that I'm very sorry for bringing shame to the family."

"Don't worry about that, son. The only one who seems concerned about that is Brenda. When you've lived as long as I have, you don't care anymore what people think."

"Thank you for saying that, Mama. I love you too much to disappoint you."

"You can never disappoint me, luv."

I heard a ruckus in the background before Aunt Brenda said, "Give me the phone, old woman. I'm tired of everyone patting him on the back." James and Olivia protested as she snatched the phone from Mama.

"Listen, you, I'm not pleased with the shame you've brought on this family. I always knew you were an auntie-man, but I preferred not to know. Now you've come out to the world. I won't be able to go shopping at Sainsbury's or even church for weeks. All our relatives are calling me from back home to know if it's true. You've made the family name a laughingstock not only back home, but everywhere else in the world we have family."

"I'm sorry—"

"Shut up! I'm not done. You need to call the press and let them know that this is not true. The auntie-men was the white boy and the African. You were just a friend of the white boy caught up in the middle of their mess."

"Oh Mum, that is ridiculous." Olivia objected. "The story is already out there. It's too late."

"No, it isn't. He's admitted to nothing. It's all speculation."

"Mum, it's easy for the press to prove that Isaiah is gay," chimed in James. "In this era of social media, that stuff is so easy to find. And trust me, there will be gay people who know Isaiah and admit that he is."

"Then he'll deny it. It's only their word against his."

I listened as the conversation went back and forth between my aunt and my two cousins, to the exclusion of me. I worried how this was making Mama feel. Aunt Brenda was really sounding ignorant, reminding me of the backwoods women back home, who thrived on gossip and superstition.

"Isaiah. I need you to do this for the family's sake."

"I'm not going to do that, Aunt Brenda."

"Why not? Boy, what is wrong with you?"

"Because it's true. I'm gay."

"Boy, what stupid-ness is this." When she was angry, she switched back to Caribbean slang.

"You just said you already knew."

"So what? Everybody don't have to."

"I won't be speaking to the press on anything, including if I'm gay."

"You going to let people speculate? You know they'll only think of the worst, which they're already doing."

"Let them speculate. I'm done trying to please people. I'm sick of it."

"Boy, you are so foolish—"

"And stop calling me boy. I'm a grown man."

"Then act like it! Put family first and stop being so selfish."

"I've always put family first; that's why I'm so screwed up."

"Don't blame us for your mess."

"But I do. I stayed in the closet out of respect for you. It has affected all my relationships, gay and straight, because I was always hiding. Afraid to admit who I truly was. All to protect a family that was more concerned with what people thought than my wellbeing."

"Now you're sounding like an auntie man, weak and pitiful."

"Then so be it. Let me enjoy being weak and pitiful in my truth instead of yours."

She hung up the phone on me. Instead of feeling hurt and

upset, I felt vindicated. I had finally stood up to my aunt after a lifetime of being respectful. I no longer felt tied to that mantle expected of Caribbean children since birth.

CHAPTER TWENTY-SIX

received a call from Terry in regards to going over my statement and coaching me for the trial. He wanted to know when I could come by the office.

I told him that I was busy at work and would not be available in the day time.

He surprised me, suggesting he'd come by my place when I got off work. I hesitated at first, but my gut was telling me, *say 'yes,' you idiot.*

Later that night, we sat at my desk in a small office area I'd created off the living room. Terry started to go over procedures and what would be expected of me, like what questions I'd be asked by the prosecutor and how to respond, how to play to the sympathy of the jury, and to be respectful of the judge. It made me think that the legal system was all a game. Whether innocent or guilty, the game had to be played, and they called this the law. I'd always wondered if, someone was guilty and there were witnesses to prove it, why was a defense lawyer needed? Why not go straight to sentencing?

After a couple of hours of that, I started to yawn. Terry took the hint to wrap things up.

"We can complete this at another time," he said.

"Good. Now can we eat this Chinese food you brought."

"Absolutely! I'm starving. Haven't eaten since midday."

"That's not good, you'll fade away."

"Nah, man. My body has gotten used to it."

I took the food out of the cardboard containers, scooping out the rice first on two plates, then putting the spicy chicken, broccoli and Chinese vegetables on top. I placed them separately in the microwave to heat.

"Would you like some wine?"

"That would be perfect."

I took out the wine Aiden had given me all those months ago. We'd never opened it. I poured some in a wine glass and took it to him.

"Where's your glass?" he asked.

"I don't drink."

"Oh really? Then what do you do to let your hair down."

"I have other means," I winked at him. He didn't get it at first. Then it dawned on him.

"Oh! Drugs. Don't tell me that, I'm your lawyer."

"I didn't, you assumed."

"Touché," he said, smiling in submission.

I brought his food and handed him a knife and fork while I settled down with my chopsticks.

"Where are my chopsticks?" he asked.

"Oh, I didn't know you knew how to use them."

"Now who's assuming."

"Touché!" we both said laughing.

I got him the chopsticks and we ate. He was very adept at handling his sticks. He looked up and smiled at me between mouthfuls. I was glad we had something so simple in common.

After dinner, we continued to sit at my small dining table, talking. Over more wine and a cup of tea for me, our conversation turned from shop to things more personal.

"Do you keep in contact with Janine?" I asked.

"Hell no! Not after what she put me through in college. Especially the pregnancy scare."

"You got her pregnant?"

"No. She lied about that."

"Why?"

"I don't know. I told you the girl was crazy."

"Then why did you stay with her."

"The sex was great."

"Of course," I responded as I took a sip of tea.

"What about you? Any crazy girlfriends back in college?"

"No. The black girls there were few and not attractive."

"What about the men?"

I quickly looked up from my cup at him. Terry was on his second glass of wine and bleary-eyed.

"What about them?"

"Any boyfriends?"

"No. I was too afraid."

"Me too."

This took me by surprise. He'd started talking about women after dinner, and I just assumed that he was straight, and I'd misjudged him.

"Was Janine a cover?"

"Yes. I didn't know what I was. I just knew I was also attracted to men."

Those beautiful brown eyes of his rested on me with more than a hint of interest. I reciprocated.

"Are you attracted to me?" I asked.

"Absolutely!" he exclaimed. "And you?"

"I guess that's an absolutely too."

Then Terry did the sweetest thing. He raised his glass in a silent toast to me. My tea mug touched his wine glass as he took my free hand in his and gently kissed it.

A few days later I asked Terry to dinner to discuss strategy in dealing with the press. I was still news—not front page, but my life still had the public's interest. God knows why, it was boring. But on occasion, he'd represent me to lessen the speculation with some made-up truths we'd concocted.

I shared with him my recent experience with my family, and the freedom I was still feeling. His expression grew empathetic as my story ended on a positive note. He congratulated me, and made a toast to my new independence.

Terry seized the opportunity to steer the conversation around to us. The feeling of guilt we both had about him being my lawyer still lingered. I often had to remind myself of what my grandmother had said, about not caring what others thought. That would temporarily work for a while, where I truly didn't care before the perceived look from a stranger made me wonder if they'd seen us on TV. I was seeing that finding my truth was not an overnight fix, and would take work.

However, there was a truth I needed to share with Terry that did haunt me. As our friendship grew, I sensed it could approach stepping over the lawyer-client boundary. I avoided being alone with him late at night, and he was beginning to notice the excuses. I had made up my mind that I would share my status with him at dinner, in the hope that he'd back off. I waited for the chance as he talked about some difficulties he was having at work with a subordinate.

I excused myself to go to the bathroom, because I saw that the issues he was ranting about would not end soon, and much of it was going right over my head. When I returned, our waiter had delivered our entrées.

"I couldn't wait. I'm hungry," Terry said, speaking to me between mouthfuls.

"That's okay. How is it?"

"This steak is delicious," he exclaimed, bringing his napkin to tap the corner of his mouth.

I watched him ravenously devour the steak. I picked at my food methodically. The food was probably very good, but I wasn't tasting it. Instead, what was marinating in my brain was how to reveal my status to this fine man. I couldn't take rejection again, but I knew it was necessary in this case. Part of me wished this wasn't developing into something, so I wouldn't have to tell and feel guilty even if we had sex. I reckoned Terry had long-term aspirations to be in a relationship, and I suspected I was a leading candidate.

"You're not eating. Is it not good?"

"It's fine. Guess I'm not hungry as you."

He took a sip of wine and looked at me with concern. It was clear he didn't believe me. Beads of sweat began to speckle my forehead.

"Something is bothering you, Isaiah. I can feel it. Won't you share it with me? Remember, it's all about living your truth now."

I tried to respond, but my mouth was suddenly feeling dry.

I took a couple gulps of water, and it helped. Terry continued scrutinizing me now with an intensity that made even more sweat flourish on my forehead.

"Terry, I want to tell you this as my lawyer, so if it comes up in the press, you're not taken by surprise."

"That you're HIV positive?" he said frankly.

"How did you know?"

"I saw the signs—it was in your actions and words. I'm a lawyer. I studied psychology before that. I'm very in tune with human behavioral patterns."

"When did you know?"

"After observing your healthy eating habits and popping pills you claimed were supplements, I began to put two and two together. But what confirmed it was when I went to throw something away in your kitchen garbage bin, and I saw a pill bottle. I could see the name partially before I pulled it out. It seemed familiar, so I googled it. That was when I knew."

It took me a moment to process this information. I didn't know whether to be relieved or angry. Both emotions battled within me.

"When did this happen?"

"About a couple of weeks ago," he said as he took another sip of wine.

He'd kept this from me for two weeks, and I had no idea. He gave no indication that anything had changed. He was professional, but showed interest in getting to know me better. I didn't have a clue that this man knew my deepest secret.

"Why didn't you say something back then?"

"Because I wanted you to."

"Were you testing me?" I said sharply.

"No, I was waiting for you to be ready."

"And what if I didn't tell you?"

"Then we'd cross that bridge if need be. But I didn't think we'd have to. I told you, I studied psychology. I pride myself on knowing human behaviors."

"Are you ever wrong?"

"Rarely."

I wanted to punch the smug look off his face. He'd strung me along for two weeks, knowing my status, waiting to see if I'd tell him. He'd snooped in my garbage and then looked up the results on Google. The battle within me was over, and anger had won. I tried to contain it as best I could. My next step surprised even me.

"I have to go." And I stood up quickly, pushing back the chair behind me. It scraped the floor harshly, drawing attention.

"What! What's the matter, Isaiah?"

"You knew and said nothing. I would think living in our truth should apply to you, too."

"If that was the case, then why didn't you tell me sooner about your truth?"

"I wasn't ready."

"That decision was not only yours to make."

"That's such a typical response from guys like you. Until you've lived this and the terrifying stigma that goes with it, you'll never understand the fear we feel to reveal it to anyone."

"Maybe not. I don't know what you've gone through. But in my world, I seek the truth. The truth always prevails. It always wins."

"This is not a trial. It's my life you're talking about."

"And mine."

I paused when he said this. There it was, out in the open. He just confirmed what he wanted from this.

He forced me to look at this from his point of view—something I hadn't really done before. Those simple two words shut it down for me. I sat back down.

"So, where do we go from here?" I asked.

CHAPTER TWENTY-SEVEN

sank into the cool folds of my therapist's leather couch and watched him take notes on a yellow manila pad. I always wondered why he didn't have a more expensive-looking notebook than that ordinary pad. He looked up, waiting for me to respond to a question he'd already asked twice—while I avoided, changed the subject or ignored it. He relentlessly came back, forcing me to say it.

"I don't know why he made me angry."

"Yes, you do," he said.

"Then maybe you should tell me, seeing as you know," I said, rolling my eyes.

"I want you to tell me. This is your journey, not mine."

I thought on what he said. Thoughts were scrambled in my brain. Making sense seemed futile. I was developing a headache. I wanted to leave, but I knew I couldn't do that. Not again. I'd come here for help.

"Maybe I was afraid."

"Afraid of what?"

"Afraid he'd still reject me for not telling him upfront."

"If that was the case then why did he wait two weeks?"

"I don't know."

"Yes, you do. Think, Isaiah!"

I looked up at the twirling ceiling fan above me as it spun around slowly. I forced myself to come up with an answer, but I was drawing a blank. My headache had gotten worse. I started to slowly deep-breathe to calm myself down, a technique my therapist had shown me. Eventually, my chest heaved a little less, and I became calmer. Out of this calm, an answer came.

"He wanted me."

"Yes, Isaiah—he wanted you and was willing to wait on you."

"Really?"

"Yes. I think so. He sounds like a patient man. Maybe that's something you need, after all you've been through. Don't throw away that opportunity."

My cousin Olivia had recently told me to not throw away the opportunity of making money and being famous. My therapist was now telling me to not throw away the opportunity of finding love. Opportunity being the operative word—I embraced that word and decided to take a chance with it.

I left my therapist's office armed with empathy, in the hope that Terry would be able to forgive me. I had told him I needed time to think this through. I'd ignored his calls. The last message he left me was that he'd wait until I was ready to talk. Now I was.

That opportunity was denied us both. Suddenly, both our schedules had filled up, making time for little else but brief texts and the occasional phone call. On the last one of those calls, I had pressed him about locating which institution Aidan was at so I could visit. He tried to talk me out of it, but backed off when he sensed it was irritating me. Finally, he texted about having found him, and wanted to know when I wanted to go visit. I told him immediately, or at least that coming Saturday, when I was off.

With Aidan on my mind for the following few days, I had become anxious. I was short with co-workers, impatient for results when they weren't even a priority. I worried about what condition he'd be in. Would he know who I was? Would he be that far gone?

Terry volunteered to go with me, even when I adamantly but politely refused. He broke me down eventually, and I agreed. Damn, he was good. He certainly chose the right profession, because his skills were obliterating my stubbornness. But what did it was that he said the long drive there would give us a chance to talk.

On the way there, Terry pulled over at a rest stop to use the bathroom. When he returned, he started the ignition, but then switched it off. He turned to me with a serious expression on his face. I knew the time had come to talk.

"How do you feel about me, Isaiah?"

"I like you Terry."

"That's it? You only like me?"

"No. More than that, but you're my lawyer."

"Don't you think I know that? It's hard, Isaiah. I'm having a hard time stifling my feelings for you. I know it's unethical and all that. I could lose my license being with you, but you're all I think about lately."

"Terry, I know. I think I want that too, but I'm still a target of the press. God forbid one of them were to find out if we had an affair. Your career would be over."

"I know. That's why I've been thinking that you should get another lawyer."

"What! Are you serious?"

"Yes, but I have a plan. Things are slowing up anyway, to where you won't need my services for some time, and when you do, I won't be available. I have a colleague I can recommend to take over your case. He's very good. You'll be in good hands. In time, we can get to know each other, and see if there's anything there without that lawyer-client tag around our necks."

"But I've come to rely on you."

"And you still can. I can advise you as a friend, even when my colleague takes over—unbeknownst to him, of course."

"I don't know, Terry. I don't want to get you in trouble if something was to go wrong."

"It won't. Trust me, I've thought this through. This is what I do for a living, leaving no stone unturned."

My whole being was flooded with conflicted emotions. I was feeling happy, yet guilty that I was about to see Aidan. I was sad that Aidan was now my past, and Terry possibly my future. Could I love Terry like I did Aidan?

I looked at Terry, and was about to respond when he gently put his finger to my lips, shushing me. Our eyes locked, and slowly, we edged closer in the car. His arms reached out and cupped my face in his hands. They trembled slightly.

The intensity of the way he looked at me was consuming, but in a good way. It was like his whole body was telling me *I got you.* I could feel myself being pulled into his energy as if by a spell.

Slowly, our lips touched, and the softness of them soothed mine, comforting me on such a deep level that I surrendered—giving myself to this man, trusting this man, caring for him, supporting him and maybe even having stronger feelings for him.

CHAPTER TWENTY-EIGHT

idan was at a mental institution in Connecticut, close to his parents' house. Silver Hill Hospital was in a huge white traditional American building with bay windows and siding, surrounded by a sprawling campus outside New Canaan. It was obviously an upscale area. It was good Aidan's parents were able to afford the best for their son.

Sitting in the crowded waiting room, I couldn't stop fidgeting. Terry looked over at me a couple of times, but didn't say anything. I was looking forward to finally seeing Aidan after all this time, but was apprehensive about the condition I might find him in. My last impression of him was not a good one. It was like his spirit had moved on, and something else inherited his body.

Every time an orderly in scrubs passed by in the hallway, I almost rose to my feet. This caused Terry to look concerned, but he still didn't say anything, on account of other people in the waiting room who weren't agitated as I was. Whoever they were visiting must be doing well, or they'd gotten used to their insanity.

No. I mustn't use that word. Aidan is not that. He just had a traumatic setback.

Finally, the orderly who had told us to sit in the waiting room came in to fetch us. I followed him first, then Terry. The guy had a big ass that practically screamed to breathe from his scrubs. He had all that equipment, yet it didn't move me like it normally would.

We passed barely-furnished rooms along the hall; some were open, with family members visiting. Towards the end of the hallway, we stopped at one door that was closed. The orderly knocked softly. There was no response, but he opened the door anyway.

We followed the orderly into the room flooded with sunlight from a large solitary window with bars. A frail figure sat on the bed with his back toward us, facing the window. I held my breath. A blanket covered his legs up to his waist. His hospital gown was tied at the back of his neck, but partially opened in the back. I could see the outline of his right scapula protruding through gaunt flesh. I stared in shock. Awkward, unsettling silence followed. I was afraid to look him in the face. I wanted to leave. *I don't think I can do this.*

The orderly, whose name was Ben, broke the silence and called out to Aidan with a friendly sense of familiarity. Aidan carefully turned around, focusing on Ben's voice with a look of anticipation in his eyes. This vanished when he saw Terry and myself standing behind Ben. I thought he was trying to register who we were.

A look of confusion shrouded his features, and his whole body slumped. Acquiescing to disorientation, he turned away from us. Ben moved to the opposite side of the bed. Facing Aidan, he leaned forward, his face silhouetted by the sun, casting a light shadow over Aidan.

"Aidan," he said, "remember I told you that you'd have visitors today? This is your friend Isaiah and a guest coming all the way from New York City to see you."

Aidan looked at Ben as if for guidance. I was still only seeing his profile. Our eyes had yet to meet. I thought he was afraid to, and I didn't know why. It was then I noticed Ben favored me a bit. Dark skin, full lips, small eyes with a bit of a slant at the ends; a bald head that was so shiny, the sun reflected off its crevice-free surface. He was Aidan's type. This revelation bothered me for a moment as I tried not to blame Aidan for who was assigned to care for him. I had to shake that feeling, realizing why I was here—it wasn't about me being in my feelings.

"Aidan, are you going to turn around and look at these nice gentlemen?"

Aidan looked down at the floor and made a sound that might have been a sigh. Ben straightened up and came around the bed back to us.

"I don't know if you're aware, but Aidan rarely speaks, and when he does, it may be a word or a sentence that we have to unscramble to know what he wants. Speech therapy has been unsuccessful so far. His progress has been little, but there is hope. The doctors say this kind of trauma can take some time to heal. There are no guarantees, but we have very good therapists here. I've seen their persistence result in miracles."

I nodded to everything he said. The realization that Aidan might never be the same hit me hard. Ben was rolling out a hopeful speech that he probably said to all family members. It seemed too rehearsed and not spontaneous. It was not doing its intended job of comforting me.

"You can talk to him, though," Ben said. "He listens. We think he understands most things. In talking to him, it may jog his memory, and if it does, you'll know. I'll give you some time to get reacquainted."

"I'll be down the hall waiting for you." Terry said, speaking for the first time. "Nice to meet you, Aidan," he said to Aidan, his words falling on deaf ears that didn't acknowledge his greeting.

They both left, closing the door softly behind them. That silent, awkward energy returned as I stood there, looking at the frail back of my friend, feeling helpless and not knowing what to say. I swiftly searched my mind for something suitable to convey.

"It's really good seeing you, Aidan. I've thought about you a lot. You look well." *I just fucked that up with that last statement.* "This is a nice place. It looks like they're treating you well here. Ben is nice. I see he's taking good care of you."

Aidan moved, adjusted his body, making himself more comfortable as the sheets surrounding him ruffled with this sudden interruption. I could still only see part of his face from the side. I saw when his eyes blinked, or his lips moved when he swallowed, and his Adam's-apple shuddered.

"I spoke to your mother. She's very nice. She wanted me to visit you. She wants all your friends to come see you," I lied again.

His mother would have nothing to do with me. I was told that she thought I was part of the reason for his relapse into this state. In her mind, I was some kind of trigger? I guess she had to blame her son's condition on someone, instead of the person in the family he'd inherited this from.

He didn't respond to my lies. He barely blinked, but stared at the wall ahead, as if he were blind. I slowly took a couple of steps to the corner of the bed, hoping that he'd look at me. But it was like I wasn't there. His green eyes looked through me, not connecting with mine. He looked tired. The permanent laugh-lines around his unsmiling face had aged him a bit.

"Aidan can I share a secret with you?" Without waiting for a response, I took a deep breath and said, "I still love you and always will."

His eyes rose to meet mine. I couldn't read what they conveyed. I was just grateful he was looking at me. He blinked a few times, and I thought I saw recognition there as his eyes opened wider slightly, and his lips attempted to smile, but didn't. I sensed he was processing what I just admitted.

"Do you remember how we first met?" I asked. "In Prospect Park, on a hot summer night. You wore all white and looked like an angel to me when I first saw you standing there, surrounded by the night. And when you hugged me, I didn't want to let go. I knew immediately you were special."

Aidan lifted his focus from mine and looked out the window into the streaming sunlight. I could tell that something registered. His eyes began to tear up, coming alive for the first time since I'd been in the room. It took human emotion and some recognition to pull him out of the trance state he was in. His smile widened a bit, though tight, without revealing his teeth. I waited and allowed him to have this moment of recollection.

I moved further around the bed, to where Ben had been, and fully faced him. The tears in his eyes multiplied as they followed me with a newfound fascination. I finally had his attention.

I reached in my pocket and pulled out his business card he'd given me. It was a little frayed around the edges from hiding in my wallet all this time. I slowly handed it to him, and he took it cautiously. Like a child, he delicately fingered the raised italic font that read, *I am the one to meet your needs.* He looked at me, and the smile widened again, just a little.

I wasn't done. I had another surprise for him, to hopefully jog his memory even further. I pulled out an envelope containing the homemade birthday card he'd given me—the one that at the time, I thought was tacky, because it was really an index card tied with coarse thread. I untied the thread and handed it to him.

He took it and opened it. He scrutinized the card as if it was a precious papyrus, bringing it close to his face and turning it over to the faded watercolors that had no meaning, but just inspired him to paint it at the time.

After he'd exhausted his investigation of the card, he leaned back in the bed and closed his eyes. I waited. Seconds turned into minutes. About five minutes later, they still remained closed, but I could see the imprint of his pupils moving. I tiptoed to the door and opened it. Ben and Terry were standing in the hallway, talking.

"Ben, I think he fell asleep."

Ben laughed. "He fell asleep on you? He does that quite often. He's past his afternoon nap."

"Okay. I wish I had a chance to say goodbye."

"You can."

"No, I don't want to wake him."

"Trust me, Isaiah, he'll fall right back to sleep after you leave."

We all went back into the room. Ben went up to the bed and leaned down over Aidan and said, "Wake up, sleepyhead. Your guests are leaving. Can you say goodbye to them?" Aidan opened his eyes, looked gingerly at Ben and then me.

"It was wonderful seeing you, Aidan. I will come and see you again soon." I found myself raising my voice, then realizing he wasn't deaf.

To my surprise, he held his hand out to me. I took his long, frail fingers, which were nicely manicured, and held them both in my hands. I could almost feel his heartbeat through his thin hands. I had tried to overlook the weight loss but it bothered me. He had a mental illness, not cancer. Why the loss?

Aidan pulled his hand from mine, and beckoned me to come close. Resting my hands on the edge of the bed, I leaned forward. He tried to say something. I could see he was wrestling with the words in his head. He eventually managed to croak out the three-syllable word, "Mar- cel." His eyes quickly searched mine for a response. I panicked and looked at Terry who mouthed to me, *tell him.*

"Aidan, Marcel is alive. He didn't die. The police captured him. He's in jail."

I expected him to freak or go into some kind of spasm but no, he didn't do that. He leaned back on the bed and smiled. Finally, I saw his teeth in a full smile. I saw a glimpse of the Aidan I knew. It made me happy to see this news bring him such joy. Ben and Terry joined him in that sentiment. Aidan closed his eyes, still smiling, and we all tiptoed out of the room.

CHAPTER TWENTY-NINE

blizzard welcomed Christmas at the end of the year. New Year's Eve was quietly spent with Terry. We celebrated the New Year with a passionate kiss under the mistletoe, which he held above our heads, and made silent wishes for the future on index cards, which we burnt outside in the snow.

Several months later, I became news again in the press. The trial date for Marcel was pending, and the press was on my tail. Terry had gotten a colleague, Sam, to represent me. He was competent enough—a chunky white male with unusually large ears. He was a stickler for details, and got me to rehearse every single scenario the prosecution could throw at me. After several weeks of this, I was sick of him, but Terry had warned me to deal with it, as he was an excellent attorney.

Terry had kept his word, and was there for me. We exchanged many intimate late-night phone calls, texts, and emails. We grew even fonder of each other from afar. We knew that we couldn't keep this up. On weekends, he'd sneak by my place around midnight, and we'd binge-watch shows on TV with a bowl of popcorn, snuggled up under a blanket on the sofa before sleep claimed us.

I liked that we weren't having sex. We were getting to know each other. This was old-school courting, and I loved it. This man was making me so happy I no longer had doubts of whether I deserved him or not.

David was the only one who knew about our union. He said it made him happy seeing how Terry had changed me. He said my essence was different. It was lighter.

Had I changed? I worried less. I didn't hold onto negatives like I used to. I seemed more grounded.

He was right. I began to notice the little things I'd taken for granted that he saw. Now I longed for the day when this trial was over, and Terry and I would no longer need to hide our relationship.

The day of the trial Sam had me do a mini rehearsal of the facts before heading to the courtroom. When we arrived, there was a huge crowd outside the courthouse. There were protestors with anti-Muslim slogans chanting "kill him" repeatedly. There were others from the Muslim community in long robes and kufi hats peering at me curiously, with curled lips of disgust. The police—some in riot gear—were in the middle, behind metal barricades that separated the two groups.

Television crews were everywhere, all broadcasting at once. Everyone was trying to be heard above the loud throngs of activity that surrounded them. When our car pulled up, the police assisted in getting us to the main entrance. A mob of reporters followed us. Even though separated behind barricades, they fired questions at Sam and snapped pictures of me. They wanted him to make a statement, but he refused by not answering them.

Inside the cool marble halls of the courthouse, I was rushed up some stairs to a private room where they kept witnesses before trial. Sam left and went into the courtroom. The deputy and I were the only people in the room. The deputy explained that other witnesses were being called; they'd let him know when it was my turn. After two cups of coffee and a Snickers bar, I was wired and ready to get this over with.

My turn eventually came like what seemed like hours later. I followed the court deputy, Frank, who'd chatted to me about football and his kids till I was sick of it. I stepped into the courtroom, and all eyes narrowed on me as the volume of chatter increased from a murmur to a ruckus. The judge stood up and banged his gavel, shouting "Order!"

He was a short, stocky man with thick black connecting eyebrows, huge, judgmental eyes, and a tiny mouth. He looked like an old grey and black night owl. He sat down once order was restored, focusing his pale face in my direction. He greeted me, his tone indifferent.

After taking the oath to tell the truth, I looked around the packed courtroom. People were even standing at the back. The faces of many strangers stared back at me. Some were indifferent; some looked at me as if I was the accused. I had been avoiding eye contact with Marcel, who sat near his lawyer. In an ill-fitting suit, obviously not his size, Marcel had cut his locks, and a bald shiny head remained. I couldn't figure out the way he was looking at me. It wasn't animosity, but I suspected it wasn't trust.

I scanned the crowd for David and found him sandwiched between a large woman and an angry-looking man, whose scowl made me wonder if it was meant for me. David nodded at me, followed by a smile of encouragement. It didn't work, because my body was feeling some kind of way. I was feeling warm in the casual wool blue suit I'd worn. My tie seemed to tighten around my neck, but I was afraid to loosen it. My back felt damp. I prayed that no one was noticing these changes in me.

I scanned the courtroom for Terry. I didn't see him. He was supposed to be here; he'd promised. *Where is he?* I found myself yelling in my head. A headache appeared out of nowhere. My hands and feet were feeling numb. I struggled to suppress nausea. I knew what was happening–I'd had these panic attacks before. I was embarrassed to be having one now. I tried with all my might to suppress it, and slowly began to breathe.

It was too late. The judge noticed my agitation and asked if I wanted a glass of water. I nodded yes. Frank the court deputy handed me a cold glass of water, which I quickly took, and poured it down my throat, attacking my anxiety into submission. That was the best glass of water I'd ever tasted. I finished the glass and handed it back to Frank. I looked up to find the collective eyes of the courtroom observing me. I bowed my head and focused on suppressing my trembling hands until I was addressed by the prosecutor.

His name was Mr. Pucket. His body had spent many decades

on the planet, but his speech, tone, and energy were that of a younger man. His opening statement was preliminary as he painted a picture of who I was and how I came to be at the scene. He was cordial to start, but as his summary progressed, his tone took on a sinister edge. Thank God Sam's opening statement was lighter, and indicated that I happened to be in the wrong place at the wrong time, before the interrogation began by the prosecutor.

"Isaiah, may I call you that?"

"Yes, sir."

"Is it correct to say that you were friends with Aidan, and not Marcel?"

"Yes sir."

"What kind of friends?"

"Objection! That is irrelevant," shouted Sam from his seat.

"I'm just trying to establish their relationship, Your Honor."

"Proceed," instructed the judge.

"Were you buddies or more?"

"More."

"And was this relationship of a sexual nature?"

"Objection! Your Honor, I don't see how this kind of detail has anything to do with what we're trying to determine here," Sam interrupted again.

The judge ignored him and waved his hand for Mr Puckett to continue.

"Do I need to repeat the question, Isaiah?"

"No sir." I swallowed hard and said, "We were intimate briefly, but then it ended, and we remained friends." There were audible rustles and disapproving groans from the courtroom as journalists furiously noted this in their notebooks or phones.

"How did you know Marcel Bahati?"

"I didn't. That was my first time meeting him that night."

"Did you know Marcel is a suspected terrorist?"

"No sir. I had no idea." I looked at David. He looked down for a moment and then looked back up at me, stone-faced.

"What was Marcel's relationship with Aidan?"

"They were old friends from when Aidan lived in Paris."

"Were they lovers too?"

I hesitated. I looked at Marcel. He sat calmly looking at me. Then, with an almost indistinguishable nod, he gave me the permission I needed.

"Yes." More groans and chatter from the courtroom, louder this time.

"Silence in the court," said the judge, banging his gavel.

"What was the imam doing there?" Mr. Puckett proceeded to ask.

"He came looking for Marcel."

"How did he know where to come?"

"I assumed Marcel told him."

"Why did he have you beaten up?"

"Because he thought I knew about *the cause.* and wanted me to confess what I knew."

"Did Aidan know about Marcel being part of the cause?"

"No."

"How do you know this for sure?"

"Because we talked about it when Marcel and the imam was in the bathroom."

"And you believed him?"

"Aidan is not one to lie. Not to me. Our relationship was special in that way."

"And you believed that, even though you were no longer his lover and not important to him?"

"Yes. I trust Aidan."

"Apparently. he didn't trust you enough to tell you that Marcel was a member of *the cause.*"

"Like I said, neither of us knew about *the cause.*"

"Don't you think that's naïve, expecting us to believe that?" Mr. Puckett said sharply.

"I do, because it's true."

Exasperated at my defiance, Mr. Puckett moved on to his next question. "Why did Marcel shoot the imam?"

"To protect us. The imam was about to shoot us because he didn't believe we knew nothing about *the cause.*"

"How come Aidan got shot and you didn't?"

"Aidan was in front of me. It all happened so fast. Marcel hesitated when the imam told him to shoot us. The imam grew angry when he didn't, and pulled out his gun and shot at us. Marcel shot him as we fell to the floor—that's when I saw that Aidan was wounded."

"What did you do then?"

"I handed Marcel duct tape to make a tourniquet to wrap around Aidan's arm to stop the bleeding."

"What about the imam?"

"He was dying and surrounded by blood. There was nothing we could do to save him. Marcel held him and prayed over him when he passed."

"It's a shame Aidan is not here to corroborate your version of the story, and it's unfortunate we will never know it from his end."

"In his current state, I don't think he could relive that again," I said sadly.

Mr Puckett's salt-and-pepper eyebrows rose in surprise. His eyes widened, startled. He looked at Sam as if for some kind of validation. Sam was shaking his head swiftly.

"It saddens me to inform the court that Aidan committed suicide earlier today. He shot himself in the head with one of his father's guns."

There was a tumultuous reaction from the courtroom. People stood up from their seats. Everyone was talking at once. Sam bowed his head. The judge banged his gavel and summoned Mr. Puckett and Sam to his chambers immediately. Journalists hurried out of the room, cellphones to their ears. The Muslims present shouted in their native tongues and dialects.

But the loudest noise that soared above the crowd was the wailing that came from Marcel. His head was on the desk, with his hands covering it. He let out guttural wails that vibrated against the desk, and his body shook with grief.

I was stunned. This was all so surreal. I watched what unfolded before me as if it was a movie, and everything was slowed down to convey the tumult and pain that came from the mouth of the prosecutor. I couldn't move, yet a calm came over me that made me rise above my incapacitation. Chaos was all around me.

The judge had given up trying to control the room. Sam quickly approached the witness stand and guided me out of it. I stepped down and looked into the eyes of Terry, collapsing in his arms as he swiftly pulled me out of there, following Deputy Frank.

CHAPTER THIRTY

woke up from a deep sleep, disoriented at first, to find I was in an unfamiliar bed. I was laying on expensive white sheets, feather pillows, and a white fluffy down comforter, in my underwear and T-shirt. I didn't want to get up, it was so comfortable, but I had to know where I was. My suit was draped across a side chair, with my shoes below it. Rising, my bare feet stepped on the cold hardwood floors. I could hear the muttering of voices in the next room.

Smiling, I recognized who the voices belonged to. I opened the door and shyly walked into the middle of their conversation. Terry and David stood up, and Terry came over to hug me. David stood behind me, giving my shoulder a reassuring squeeze.

"Are you okay, Isaiah?" Terry asked as he planted a gentle kiss on my forehead.

"Yes, I think so."

"Are you hungry, honey?" David asked.

"No. But I'd love a cup of coffee."

"Coffee coming up," David said, giving me one more reassuring pat before heading to the kitchen.

"Your place is lovely," I told Terry.

"Thank you."

"It's nice. It's very you. Classic and tasteful."

"Well thank you, sir. I appreciate that, coming from you. A man of the highest taste." He pecked me gently on the lips.

"Ugh! Don't do that. I'm sure I have morning breath."

Terry shrugged and hugged me tighter. We held each other quietly until my coffee arrived.

"Come on you lovebirds. Get a room!" David joked.

Terry reluctantly released me so I could wrap my forefinger around the handle of the mug and take my first sip. It was delicious. David made the best coffee—just like I liked it, dark and sweet.

"That tastes so good. Maybe it will wake me up. I feel groggy."

"That's because of the two sleeping pills I gave you."

"So, what were you two talking about before I came in?" I asked.

"The game."

"What, you, David?" I said, amused.

"Men in tights and shoulder pads turn me on," he giggled. "But we were also talking about you."

"Oh lawd!" I exclaimed. "What did I do now?"

"Nothing, honey. I was just thanking Terry for all he's done for you, and I think," he hesitated before proceeding, "that he's good for you, and I hope he's the one, because honey, I'm tired of babysitting you. It's time for you to be someone else's responsibility." We all burst out laughing, and I reached over and hugged him.

"I'm tired of you too, honey," I sneered playfully.

Our conversation soon drifted to other subject matters. We avoided what was uppermost in our minds. The time was not right to spoil this moment of bliss with my two favorite men.

Reality has a way of inserting itself back into your life when you don't want it to. Aidan's death delayed the trial from being completed. Sam was doing his best to make sure I wouldn't have to testify anymore. I wasn't looking forward to facing the formidable Mr. Puckett again, but somehow, I knew that was inevitable.

Marcel's fate still had to be determined. He killed a man in self-defense of us, based on my testimony, and faced a manslaughter charge. However, there were some pending charges overseas in regards to him being present at executions carried out by *the cause.* He could face extradition to France. Terry told me Marcel had not taken Aidan's death well. He'd fallen into a deep depression and gone on a hunger strike, losing his appetite but not in protest. Terry assumed it was over, because this happened weeks ago.

Terry and I were dating, and so far, it was going well. We were both living our truth and had found it in each other. I relished each moment I spent with this special man, and missed him when I was away from him. He got me and I got him. We were accepting of our shortcomings with humor, and didn't take ourselves seriously, because the end result was too great to mess up. I was finally beginning to know what being truly happy was. We were planning a trip together. I couldn't leave the country, so we settled for Miami, Florida.

I couldn't wait, and went shopping for new shorts, swimwear, tank tops, and a pair of flip-flops. This new wardrobe was to complement the new me and the new chapter in my life I was embarking on. I hadn't felt this excited about going away in a long time, and this was going to be the romantic vacation I'd always dreamed of with Mr. Right.

I spoke to almost everyone in my family after the courtroom fiasco, except for Aunty Brenda. She was still mad at me for shaming the family and my story being front-page news worldwide. I hoped she would get over it in time, but knowing her, she didn't let go of grudges easily. I would have to learn to forgive her for my sake.

The love I got from Mama extinguished my aunt's negativity. Mama told me she prayed for my safety while keeping me in her thoughts and dreams. I couldn't ask for more than that from this amazing woman. I pledged to keep in touch more often, and to visit soon. I worried that her time with us was numbered, and due to my own fears, I'd already missed too many years of loving her back.

David was dating a new man. He wouldn't tell me who it was because it was in the early stages. He said it was someone he'd met during the whole process of me being in jail and the trial. They'd hit it off and found they had a lot in common. He wasn't sure initially if the man was gay until the man asked him out for a date. I was so happy for him and hoped it worked out. I'd eased off pressuring him and waited till he was ready to reveal who the mystery man was.

Finally, the day of our trip to Miami came: five glorious days of sun, romance, cocktails, and hot sex. Terry arrived at my apartment to pick me up, and of course, I wasn't ready.

"Babe, you had weeks to pack," he said, impatiently looking at his watch.

"I know but I changed my mind about what I wanted to bring."

"We're only going for five days, not two weeks," he said, smirking at my luggage.

"Give me a moment; I'm almost done."

"Okay," he said and turned on the TV.

I was in the bathroom when I heard him calling me to come quickly. "Babe, I think you need to check out this breaking news."

When I entered the living room, Marcel's face was on the TV. It was the same picture I had made a copy of. They were talking about his time in Paris and his association with *the cause.*

I sat down next to Terry and focused on the caption below the anchorman. TERRORIST MARCEL BEHATI FOUND DEAD IN CELL. I looked at Terry in disbelief. The anchorman ended the breaking news and moved on to another headline.

"He hanged himself. They think it's suicide, but they have to do an investigation," Terry said, filling me in.

Do you think the depression caused this?"

"It's most likely. Aidan's death hit him hard. Sadly, all he had to look forward to was many years in prison. Let me call Sam for more details. Babe, we gotta go."

While Terry got on his cellphone to Sam, I went into the bedroom to see if I'd forgotten anything. Still shocked about Marcel, even though I didn't know the guy, I had to admit I'd come to admire him for not only saving our lives, but being a gay Muslim and living it, even though it was on the DL.

I continued checking my list to see if I'd forgotten anything, then I noticed I'd missed checking off my watch. I opened the bedside table drawer to retrieve it from the box it came in, compliments of Terry. I noticed the edge of a picture was peeping out from underneath it. I pulled it out and looked at the picture of Aidan and I that David had taken at the Jazz Festival in Thompson Square Park. It made me smile. We looked so happy, and for a while, I reminisced about that sunny day when my feelings grew for this man. It was one of the few times I saw him really relaxed and happy. Staring at the picture, those feelings came rushing back to me. I found myself speaking out loud to it.

"He's with you now. You're together again. I tried to make you love me, but he was the one that filled your heart. I still love you, though, and thank you for being the cause of that experience."

The door to my bedroom creaked open. Terry stood at the door. His expression was sad and dejected.

"The taxi is here. See you downstairs," he said coldly, and left.

I took one more look at the picture before returning it to the drawer. I paused before closing my apartment door, wondering if I'd ever get over Aidan and would a remnant of him remain? It wasn't fair to Terry; I knew, but I hoped in time I'd come to love him in that way, too—if he'd still have me.

ABOUT THE AUTHOR

Hello to all,

I am a passionate writer of gay stories that touch on real social issues and inner conflict that confront gay black men. My aim is to engage the reader; entertain, arouse, move, and think. I hope that my stories leave an aftertaste and the urge to want more. They touch on a variety of topics that include: love, dating, sex, health, homophobia, aging, depression, religion, politics and much more. My other books are; Phat Boi, Encounters of Passion, The Little Red Slip.

Happy Reading,

Aaron Blackwood

Follow me on:

- Facebook (personal page) https://www.facebook.com/aaron.blackwood.77

- Facebook (author page) https://www.facebook.com/TheWriterAaronBlackwood/

- Twitter **@1AaronBlackwood**

- Website http://aaronblackwood.com/